Personal Best

Personal Best

Sylvia Gunnery

James Lorimer & Company Ltd., Publishers
Toronto

James Lorimer & Company Ltd. acknowledges the support of the Ontario Arts Council. We acknowledge the support of the Government of Canada through the Book Publishing Industry Development Program (BPIDP) for our publishing activities. We acknowledge the support of the Canada Council for the Arts for our publishing program. We acknowledge the support of the Government of Ontario through the Ontario Media Development Corporation's Ontario Book Initiative.

Cover illustration: Greg Ruhl

The Canada Council | Le Conseil des Arts
for the Arts | du Canada

ONTARIO ARTS COUNCIL
CONSEIL DES ARTS DE L'ONTARIO

Library and Archives Canada Cataloguing in Publication
Gunnery, Sylvia
    Personal best / Sylvia Gunnery.

(Sports stories ; 81)
ISBN-13: 978-1-55028-897-1 (bound)
ISBN-10: 1-55028-897-0 (bound)
ISBN-13: 978-1-55028-896-4 (pbk.)
ISBN-10: 1-55028-896-2 (pbk.)

    I. Title. II. Series: Sports stories (Toronto, Ont.) ; 81
PS8563.U575P47 2005   jC813'.54   C2005-904857-3

James Lorimer & Company Ltd.,
Publishers
317 Adelaide Street West
Suite 1002
Toronto, Ontario, M5V 1P9
www.lorimer.ca

Distributed in the United States by:
Orca Book Publishers
P.O. Box 468
Custer, WA USA
98240-0468

Printed and bound in Canada.

Contents

Acknowledgements

I have thoroughly enjoyed working with my editor, Hadley Dyer, who likes the Hirtle family as much as I do and who mixes friendly humour with her "tough editor's veneer."

If not for a timely visit from Buck Simm and his big brother Greg, I wouldn't have known about Spud Webb, and this book may have been stalled forever at chapter 5.

For Mom, in her 90th year;
and for my sister, Barbara

1

Out of Control

From the bedroom window, Jay watched Gramp tie three balloons to the mailbox post at the end of the lane. They were Canada Day balloons, white with splashes of red. It made him smile because Gramp wasn't really a balloon kind of guy.

He picked up his backpack and his duffle bag full of sports gear, including the white-and-blue sneakers his dad and mom had given him on his last day at Centreville School. They were celebration sneakers, double time. Jay had played on the Centreville basketball team when they won the Junior Boys' Western Division Championship. He scored eight points and had no fouls. Not one. The other reason for the new sneakers was that Jay was going to his first summer basketball camp.

Jay's little brother Sam had been given a two-wheeler with gold streamers on the handlebars. That bike was a celebration gift, too, because kindergarten was now history and Sam was on his way to Grade 1. He wasn't having much fun on his new bike, though. Potholes were like a plague of zits all over the road in front of Gramp's. Back home in Richmond, he would be flying down the smoothly paved street with those gold streamers flapping, his hair sticking straight up over his forehead, and maybe even a few bugs mashed on his front teeth.

In about two weeks, the repairs from February's fire dam-
age as well as all the renovations would be completed. Finally,
the Hirtle family would be able to move from Gramp's in Centreville back to their own home in Richmond.

"Ready for basketball camp?"

"Yeah."

"Did you pack extra socks and—"

"I've got everything I need, Mom. Honest. And Dad gave
me some money in case I run out of anything or whatever."

"Let's run out now," said Sam through a mouthful of toast.

"No time, big guy. Besides, you always win."

"You let me win."

"Not every time. Get Dad to race with you today."

"We're going to the perrade, Rudy, too."

Rudy lifted his head off his paws and thumped his large tail
on the kitchen floor.

"Maybe not, Rudy, sweetie," said Mrs. Hirtle. "You know
how much he howls at the bagpipes."

"And he'd chase after those batons when the majorettes hurl
them up in the air. I swear Rudy's mental," Jay added.

The dog's eyes went from one person to the next, following
the mention of his name as if they were throwing a bright yellow ball from hand to hand.

"I can hold on tight."

"Right. And when Rudy gets it in his head to chase one of
the floats, you'll be flapping like a flag at the end of that leash.
Everyone'll think you guys are part of the parade. Clowns. Sam
and his mental German shepherd, Rudy. Better wear a red ball
on your nose, buddy."

Sam touched the end of his nose. He touched Rudy's nose,
too. Then he gave the dog the last corner of his toast.

The cellphone on the kitchen table chimed a tinny version

of the theme for *Hockey Night in Canada*.

"Who's been messing with my phone again?"

"Um, that'd be the hospital callin', Mom," said Jay. He winked at Sam.

"Hello. Dorothy Hirtle." She walked out of the kitchen and into the quiet of the living room where her husband was still sleeping on Gramp's Hide-A-Bed.

"That call's probably about one of her patients," said Jay. "Maybe Mom won't get to catch the parade."

"I can catch the perrade. I can bring it home and she can watch it after."

"You're as mental as that dog, big guy."

"Are there tents at basketball camp?"

"There's dorms. Like with beds and closets. Mike and me'll be roommates, just like you and me here at Gramp's."

"Can Rudy sleep in your bed?"

"Sure. He'll be your roommate while I'm away."

Sam patted Rudy's head thoughtfully. "Roomdog."

Since Jay had found out he had been accepted at Basketball Nova Scotia's summer camp, he'd been checking off the days on the calendar. Finally, July 1st was here.

It was going to be so cool. Guys from all over Nova Scotia would be on the Acadia University campus together for a week, trying out the moves they hoped would give them the edge when they played for their schools next season.

Mrs. Hirtle came back into the kitchen. "I'm going over to the hospital to check on Mary Hebb. Her water broke, but she won't be delivering that baby for quite a while yet."

"Rudy's water broke," said Sam. "When he was little."

"Drink your milk, Sam. And then get out of those PJs. I'll meet you and Dad on King Street before the parade starts. Don't forget your hat."

"Rudy, too?"

"Rudy will stay here with Gramp. He'll be happier. Less noise and less heat."

"Hey, there's Mike and Chad." Jay opened the side door and shouted. "Hi you guys! I'm almost ready! Come on in while I get my stuff!"

Rudy squeezed in beside Jay and poked his nose out through the door, wagging his large tail.

Mike stepped into the kitchen, his head just barely making it under the door frame. His older brother, Chad, was right behind him and almost as tall. Jay always felt like he was overdue for a growth spurt whenever he stood next to these two guys.

"You boys have breakfast?" asked Mrs. Hirtle.

"Mom stuffed us with sausages and eggs and waffles," said Chad. "She thinks we're driving to Texas."

"Is Texas far?" said Sam.

"Farther than Wolfville."

"Rudy's my roomdog."

"He means roommate, sort of." Jay passed his backpack to Mike. "Put this in the car for me, will ya? I gotta go say bye to Dad."

"Here's some bottled water. One for each of you," said Mrs. Hirtle. "Nice and cold for the trip."

"Thanks," said Mike. "It's gonna be muggy. Feels like thunder."

Mike and Chad went to the car. Jay came back downstairs and into the kitchen.

"Make sure you say goodbye to your grandfather. He's down on the wharf. Come here first. Give your mother a kiss."

"I'm going down the wharf, too," said Sam, sliding off his chair.

"You're going upstairs to get dressed. Right now. Give your big brother a hug and some advice for his first long trip away from home."

Jay bent down so Sam could plant a bear hug around his neck. "So big guy, what's your advice?"

"Um," Sam's eyes slid up and sideways as if he were trying to look inside his mind for something wise to say. "Um. Don't pee in your bed!" he shouted and then laughed hysterically.

"You crack me up, Sam."

When Jay had said goodbye to Gramp and walked back from the wharf, he felt a pinch of loneliness. He gave a last wave to his mom and dad, who were standing at the door. Sam was upstairs in the bedroom window, knocking on the glass. Rudy was beside him, his paws on the window ledge. Jay waved to them. He was only going about two hours away. It wasn't like it was the other side of the universe. And it would just be for a week. But still …

"Here's some water your mom gave us." Mike handed the cold plastic bottle to Jay when he got into the back seat.

As Chad eased his old car to the end of the lane and signalled left, Jay took a close look at the three balloons Gramp had tied to the mailbox post. The red splashes were maple leaves. There were a couple of big ones and then smaller and smaller ones, like they were being blown far away by a sudden blast of wind. He thought of Gramp struggling with those balloons, blowing them up and then tying them in place. His large, rough hands, used to heavy rope and fishing line, would have been awkward for this new task.

The lonely feeling pinched a bit sharper in Jay's chest.

Though he didn't know it yet, Jay was going to return to Gramp's in less than a week's time—before summer basketball camp was even over. On the long drive from the hospital in

Kentville to Gramp's in Centreville, he and his dad would have plenty of time for explanations about the accident, and for serious conversation about whether Mike would be okay. Jay would look through the darkness at Gramp's mailbox, no longer decorated with balloons. He would wish it was Canada Day again, and that life was still as simple as three white balloons splashed with red maple leafs.

"Basketball camp's gonna be a blast!" yelled Chad over the car stereo.

"Do you get to pick your team? It'd be cool if me and Jay could be on your team."

"They'll have all that worked out before we get there. Maybe they don't let brothers coach brothers, though. Hey, what's with this guy in front of us? Sightseeing or what?" Chad stepped on the gas and started to pass. Jay noticed the broken highway line had change to a double yellow one. Ahead of them was a sharp curve where the highway disappeared from sight. No traffic was coming yet. Chad pulled back into the right lane just as a truck came into sight up ahead.

Soon the slower car was far behind them. Jay relaxed in the back seat, thinking about basketball camp and feeling pretty good breezing along the highway with Chad and Mike.

Fog began to billow like smoke in front of them. From the top of the hill there was usually a view of the small islands scattered along the coast. Today there was only a grey wall of fog. Hundreds of spider webs outlined with silver beads of dew were draped from spruce trees like someone's idea of a Halloween joke. Dark clouds overhead seemed ready to burst with rain. Jay hoped it wouldn't rain on Richmond's Canada Day parade.

At exit 9, they turned onto the secondary highway that would take them across the province to the Annapolis Valley.

Jay was thinking that, with the speed limit reduced to 90 k.p.h., Chad's foot might not get another chance to turn into a boulder on the gas peddle.

About twenty kilometers later, a motorcycle came up behind them. The chainsaw buzz of the motor drowned out the car stereo as the bike roared past with two loud revs.

"Let's get this guy," said Chad.

Mike grinned.

Jay pictured Chad's foot turning into a boulder.

"We'll get him going up that hill. That thing doesn't have the guts this car's got." He stepped on the gas and a billow of bluish-grey smoke puffed out a protest from the muffler. When they caught up to the bike, Chad gave a blast on the horn and passed him. "See ya, sucker!"

Mike tuned around and waved as they sped past, still grinning wildly.

Jay felt trapped. Right now, he'd rather be anywhere but in the back seat of Chad's old wreck of a car. Any place where he might have at least a bit of control over the situation.

The guy on the motorcycle obviously had a problem with tailing in someone else's exhaust, just like Chad did. But he didn't drop back to avoid the fumes. He was trying for a chance to gain the lead.

Up ahead was a car following a truck.

"Oh, right. That's all we need," said Chad. "That truck's towing the damn car."

The chainsaw sound of the bike kept roaring, then hushing, roaring and hushing, impatient behind them.

"This idiot thinks he's gonna pass us again. I don't believe it." Chad pressed hard on the gas pedal.

The guy behind them took the challenge and opened up the throttle. The bike roared past. It roared even louder as it zoomed ahead of the car and then the truck, moving around a corner and out of sight.

"Damn!" There was too much length of car and rope and truck ahead of them and too little visible road. Chad couldn't chance a pass. He slammed hard on the brakes, laying a licorice ribbon of rubber. His old car fishtailed.

Jay's body was flung to the right and then the left, straining against his seatbelt.

Finally, Chad regained control of his car. No vehicles were behind them. None were coming toward them. Lucky again, thought Jay. Very lucky.

They could hear the fading sound of the bike far ahead of them. The truck continued towing the car in its slow, purposeful way, as if the driver hadn't even noticed the squeal of tires.

"Well, that was a bit of excitement," said Chad, laughing.

Mike looked at his older brother and grinned. He obviously wasn't thinking the same thing Jay was thinking: *What's with Chad? Why's he acting like such a jerk? What next?*

Jay's heart started to settle back down. For a minute there, it had been just about in his throat. He straightened his seatbelt and picked up the bottle of water from the floor.

If basketball camp was going to be anything like the drive to get there, it sure wasn't going to be dull.

2

Tornadoes

Which side d'you want?" asked Mike.

"Whatever. Doesn't matter."

Jay and Mike were standing in the doorway of the room they would share for the next week. On each side of the large window were identical desks made from some kind of cheap wood. Wooden chairs with no cushions sat beside the desks. There were two bunks that had drawers underneath, and two closets that didn't have much room inside. The green paint was chipped where posters, pictures, and other memorabilia had been nailed or taped to the walls.

"Okay then, I'll take this side." Mike threw his stuff on a bed.

Jay sat on the other bed. "Mattress must be made of plywood." He stood up and went to the window. It was still a grey day, but so far no rain.

Their room was on the third floor of Chipman House, one of the oldest dorms at Acadia University. Outside, Jay could see a few summer students in quiet spots on the acres of lawn. They were leaning against massive oak and maple trees, trying to soak up information from textbooks the size of suitcases.

A convertible blasting music pulled into the parking lot beside Chipman House. Two girls were inside. Within seconds, two guys appeared, and, after a bit of a shuffle, one couple jumped into the back and a guy slid into the passenger seat. The car took off.

A van drove into the parking lot and stopped. The two occupants stayed inside and talked for a few seconds. Then the passenger got out, shut the door, and didn't look back. He leaned forward under the weight of his overstuffed backpack. Red, mid-cut basketball sneakers hung from one of the straps. Obviously another guy arriving for basketball camp.

This whole campus scene was one big excitement for Jay.

Chad opened their door and walked in. "You guys figure everything out? Washrooms, TV lounge, stuff like that?"

"Pretty much," said Mike.

The guy with the backpack and red sneakers walked past their opened door.

"Hey," said Chad, stepping out into the hall again. "Now, you've gotta be a basketball player. And I'm not just talking about those red sneakers. What's your name?"

The backpack and red sneakers stopped and the guy turned around. "Martin." He looked down at Chad from about a three-inch height advantage. His brown eyes gave a steady stare, and he wasn't smiling. He wore an oversized Chicago Bulls' T-shirt with the sleeves cut out and black baggy shorts. A shadow of black hair covered his shaved brown head.

"Where you from, Marty?"

"Martin. No 'y'."

"Right."

"Halifax."

"Halifax? Lotta great ball players come from there."

There was something about Martin that Jay liked right away, despite the steady stare and no smile. He didn't look unfriendly, exactly. He just wasn't giving his friendship away for free. *Martin. No 'y'.* It was cool the way he'd said that. He looked older, maybe sixteen. Jay had to agree with Chad—Martin did have the look of a basketball player. Tall. Sure of himself. And he worked out, obviously.

"What's your room number?" asked Jay.

"307."

"That's right beside us. My name's Jay and this is Mike."

"Who's your roommate gonna be?" asked Mike.

"Don't know. Doesn't matter."

"Doesn't matter? You've gotta be kidding," said Chad. "You're gonna share that room for a whole week, hear the guy snore all night, trip over his dirty clothes on the floor, listen to whatever crap music he likes, even if he's got headphones, and you think it doesn't matter who your roommate is?"

Martin just shrugged his shoulders. Then he walked into room 307 and closed the door.

"What's with him?" said Chad. "Whoever coaches that guy's gonna have trouble on his hands."

"Bet he knows basketball," said Jay.

"Skill's second to attitude. Anyway, the guy's not my problem. I've got a coaches' meeting right now. You guys have to be down at the gym in an hour, right?"

Acadia's gymnasium was like the inside of an airport terminal compared to the junior high gyms Jay was used to. There were enough bleachers here to hold the entire town of Richmond. When he looked up into the steel rafters, the back of his neck kinked. He felt weird inside this cavernous place. Small weird. Vole-sized.

The head coach was greeting everyone as they came out of the locker room and into the gym. "Welcome to Basketball Nova Scotia's summer camp! Find yourselves a spot on the floor and relax."

The guys looked ready to work up a sweat. Everyone was wearing basketball shorts and T-shirts, some cut off at the shoulders and some with a school crest or a company logo. Most guys had short hair or shaved heads, and the ones who had longer hair were wearing sweatbands to keep it out of their faces. Quite a few players looked like they had high school basketball experience. Jay even wondered if maybe he and Mike were the only players who weren't in high school yet.

Sitting in the bleachers were about a dozen junior coaches who were over nineteen and still played for university teams. They all wore white Basketball Nova Scotia coach's shirts. Chad was sitting at the end of the front row.

"We're here at this basketball camp for two equally important reasons," said the head coach, after everyone had settled down. "This is an opportunity for you players to pick up some of the best skills and strategies you'll see on any basketball court anywhere. At the same time, this is an opportunity for these junior coaches to hone their game skills and their people skills, and to set themselves up for a career in coaching. They already know the main thing coaching's all about, and that's you, the players. A coach's job is to pull a team together, create a basketball family and, within that family, lead every single basketball player toward achieving his personal best. A coach is a role model on and off the court. A coach is an adviser on and off the court."

A couple of the junior coaches started to clap and then everyone else got into it.

The head coach didn't crack a smile. "Coaching's not an easy job. There'll be obstacles. Some players won't be accurate with shots, or quick on the rebound, or fast with passes. There's going to be conflict. Between players. And between players and coaches. There's going to be victory. There's going to be defeat.

When there's victory, props will go to the players. When there's defeat, it's the coaches who'll take the heat. That's what the job's all about."

Jay looked over at Chad and saw that he was rubbing his fingertips along the small square of hair sprouting below his lower lip. He didn't look too excited about all that conflict-defeat talk.

"And you basketball players have a big job, too," continued the head coach, his hands on his hips. "Listen up when your coach speaks. Do what he says. It'll be for your own good and for the good of the whole team. Give everything your best shot. No coach can ask more than that."

"But first things first. We've got some terrific T-shirts for all of you from all of us at Basketball Nova Scotia. Get yourselves sorted into lines. I've got the large and extra large sizes. Mediums and smalls line up over there."

Mike headed for the large and extra large line, while Jay got in the line for a medium. He took a close look at the T-shirt and liked everything about it. It was white cotton, and across the front was a large Basketball Nova Scotia logo: blue waves, a white sailboat, and a large basketball like a bright orange sun rising behind the boat. Cool.

When everyone had been given a T-shirt and had sat back down on the floor, the head coach held his hands up for quiet. "Okay, I want you to put your hands together for Basketball Nova Scotia Summer Camp's assistant coach, Jamie Clark."

The gymnasium thundered with applause. Jamie was about twenty-five years old with long arms and legs—a bonus for any basketball team.

"What a bunch of keeners! Great!" He waited for the clapping to die down. "There's lots planned for our week together. Five days of drills and instruction and practice. Then, as you

already know, we'll be hosting a weekend basketball tournament. Three university alumni teams—Acadia, Saint Mary's,
and Dalhousie—will display the best ball in our province. In all
of Canada. Six of you will earn the chance to play on those
alumni teams in the tournament. Two on each team."

Jay nudged Mike, who sat on the floor beside him. "That'll
be you, I bet."

"Or you," said Mike.

"Fat chance." But Jay smiled anyway. They hadn't even
started to play basketball yet, but maybe it wouldn't be impossible. Maybe he had just as much chance of playing in the
weekend tournament as any other guy here. No sense giving up
before he even started.

"My message to you today is three-sided," said Jamie, walking over to a flip chart. He picked up a thick blue marker. "Think
of a triangle, all sides equal." He drew a wobbly blue triangle on
the flip chart. "If you want to make changes to your basketball
game—" now he picked up a red marker, "—you have to be
ready mentally ..." He put a gigantic M on one blue line. "And
you have to be ready emotionally ..." Now a red E. "Then you
have to be ready physically." A red P was scrawled across the
third side of the triangle. "Think about it." He tapped the marker
against the M. "Whatever goal you set for yourself, whatever
change you want to make, it means your head has to believe you
can do it." He moved the marker to the E. "And you have to put
your whole heart into it. That's the emotional side." Now the
marker pointed to the P. "And you won't change anything about
your basketball game unless your body knows exactly how to
execute the manoeuvres. That's the physical part of the job." He
waited half a second for all that to sink in. "Mental. Emotional.
Physical." The marker tapped its way around the triangle.

"Jamie's one hundred percent right on all three pointers

there," said the head coach, stepping up beside his assistant. "I've seen it many, many times. A player wants to improve his game say, for example, his shot form. He knows in his mind this will enhance his game, earn his team more points. He's pumped for it, willing to practice for hours on end, one shot after another. So, mentally and emotionally the player's prepared for change. But, say this player isn't paying attention to his coach. Or maybe he doesn't quite understand his coach's instructions about finding balance, knowing the target, following through. Then this player isn't physically ready to improve his basketball skills."

The gym became so quiet it felt like it was empty. Every player was thinking silent thoughts about that blue triangle and the gigantic red letters—M, E, and P. To Jay, even though he'd never thought of it that way, the whole thing about that triangle made a lot of sense. He had a feeling this idea would pay off for him, big time. M: mental. E: emotional. P: physical. Right.

"Okay, now!" shouted Jamie. "Let's see what you boys are made of! Take it around the outside!"

All the players got up and put their new T-shirts on the bleachers. Then they started jogging around the perimeter of the gym. The junior coaches watched from the sidelines, some clapping their hands with encouragement and some, like Chad, folding their arms across their chests, frowning thoughtfully.

Jay slipped into the stream of runners and tried to hit a good stride. It took him approximately half a second to realize that he was just about the shortest basketball player there. On the Rockets basketball team, and also with the Centreville Cougars last season, Jay had measured in at about average height. Height didn't really matter much when he was dunking high scores most games anyway. But here things felt different.

Mega-different. And he was probably the youngest guy, too. The summer basketball camp had been advertised for ages thirteen to sixteen. If anyone else was thirteen, they were doing a good job of hiding it. He could feel the E side of that blue triangle fading fast.

Mike jogged past him.

He started thinking about a little guy in Grade 7 at Richmond Academy who had tried out for the Rockets basketball team last September. At less than five feet, he didn't have a chance. Some of the guys nicknamed him Hamster and joked about his short legs. Coach Willis had taken him aside, eventually, and dropped a few gentle hints about how basketball players needed at least some height and speed. Next practice, the little guy wasn't there. No matter how much M and E he might've had, he didn't have the physical ability to play the game.

Martin jogged past Jay.

Two more runners made a detour around Jay and ran ahead. His breath was coming in small bursts, now, and his heart rate shot up.

In what seemed like only minutes, Martin passed him again. Then Mike came running along just behind Martin.

A cluster of guys almost got tangled up in the roadblock Jay was making. One runner told him, "Pick it up, pick it up." Another one brushed against his shoulder, just about knocking him off balance. He couldn't stop thinking about that little guy in Grade 7. Now he knew exactly how that kid must have felt.

The muscles at the tops of Jay's legs tightened. Sweat trickled down his face and glued his hair to his forehead. His chest heaved with each gasp.

A whistle blew, finally. The runners slowed to a stop. A few did some leg stretches and some just leaned over to get their breathing under control. Jay's face felt red hot and ready to boil over.

The head coach called out names from a clipboard. Each coach would get six players: a line and a spare. "Coach Anderson. These are your players: Saunders, Boyd, Murphy …"

The sorting went on until it was Chad who stepped forward to meet his team. The third name called was Hirtle. Chad would be Jay's coach.

Jay found himself making a mental list. *Things to feel weird about at basketball camp*:

1) being thirteen, almost fourteen, when most guys were sixteen or at least looked like it, 2) being five-seven when most guys were at least six feet, and 3) just about coughing up a gut from running around a monster-sized gym.

The list was very likely going to get longer. Jay tried to forget all the letters of the alphabet except M, E, and P.

Martin's name was called for Chad's team, too. He loped across the gym and stood with the rest of the guys. Jay was about to say "Hey, Martin!" and give him a high-five. But Martin didn't look like he was up for much team-spirit stuff.

"I gotta say," said Chad. "I lucked out. Watching you guys run those laps was proof enough for me. You guys are championship material."

Jay could see right through Chad's pep talk. *Build 'em up. Keep 'em positive. Lie, lie, lie.* Or maybe he'd been wearing a blindfold when Jay had slogged past. And had he already forgotten the stuff he'd said about how Martin would probably be trouble for whoever coached him?

Chad picked up a basketball and rolled it between his palms. "Let's make a circle and get to know this ball. I want to see snap passes and quick reflexes. You know the drill."

The basketball snapped from Chad to Steve, from Steve to Martin, from Martin to Jay. The tight roundness of that orange ball, the small bumps, were familiar in Jay's hands. His pass to

Chris was fast and sure. Jay felt like a basketball player again.

Then Chad set them up for a two-on-one drill. "Steve, Brent, Martin. You're up. The rest of you, have a seat for a few minutes. Okay guys, show your stuff."

Chad moved around the players, shouting, "Where's the hoop?" and "Go for two!" and "Rebound! Rebound!"

After a few minutes, Chad took Brent and Martin off the floor and played in Chris and Ronny. The next switch saw Brent and Martin back in and Steve and Chris on the bench beside Jay.

Soon Chad stopped the basketball action. The gym still echoed with sounds of other teams and their coaches. "It's a start, guys. It's a start. Take a break." Then he looked over at Jay. "Hey, man. I forgot to play you in. Sorry 'bout that. I'll get you next time."

Another item was added to Jay's *Things to feel weird about* list:

4) having a coach with memory deficiencies.

"Okay, guys," said Chad. "Let's talk. Have a seat. Now, we need a team name. I thought about Cheetahs. Chad's Cheetahs."

"That's lame."

Chad looked over at Martin, who stood with one foot on the bench.

"You got a better suggestion?"

"Nope."

"Then maybe you need to think instead of criticize, Marty."

"Martin."

"Right. Forgot. And like I said, have a seat."

Martin waited a second before he moved his foot from the bench and sat down, still keeping eye contact with Chad.

Jay tried his suggestion. "How about Dolphins?"

"Or Elks," said someone else.

"Does it have to be animals? What about Hurricanes?"

"Typhoons."

"Tornadoes."

"Blizzards."

"I like Tornadoes," said Chad. "Sounds powerful. Ominous, like the other teams better know we're comin'. Who votes for Tornadoes?"

Most hands went up.

"Okay. We're the Tornadoes. Now, let's get some more action here. Martin, you're on the bench. Steve and Ronny, too."

Jay wasn't fooled. He knew Chad wasn't trying to be fair by playing him now. He was sending Martin a clear message about who was in control. The Tornadoes would be a perfect name for this team—some kind of big storm was obviously not far off, maybe a violent one.

Most of the guys were hyped heading back to the dorm at the end of that first practice, . Some of them were already wearing their Basketball Nova Scotia T-shirts. Even the muggy, grey July afternoon couldn't smother the excitement.

Jay could see the top of Mike's curly hair as he walked with a group of guys about half a block away. Mike was definitely one of the tallest players at this basketball camp, just like he was back home in Centreville. Lucky him. But he wasn't so lucky when it came to brothers. Jay definitely had better luck than Mike in the brother category.

That night, when the lights were turned off and Jay had found a semi-comfortable spot on the plywood mattress and paper-thin pillow, he thought about home. Well, not home exactly, but Gramp's.

Right now, Gramp might be sitting in the kitchen eating toast and drinking tea before going to bed. Sam would be asleep for sure, wearing his favourite Spider-Man pajamas and all tangled up in his sheets. Rudy would be sprawled on Jay's bed, across the room from Sam, his large paws twitching as he chased the neighbour's black cat in his dream. Jay's mom and dad would be watching the news on TV, or more likely talking about the renovation they were doing on their fire damaged house.

He didn't actually want to be back at Gramp's, but it gave Jay a nice feeling to make this family movie in his head. It was a much better movie than the one about him jogging around the gym wearing brick sneakers, or the one about him sitting on the bench being ignored by his basketball coach.

3

Secrets

A thin fog had crept in off the Bay of Fundy and settled across the Acadia University campus early by the next morning. Soon, the heat would burn the fog away and the July day would be a scorcher. But now it was cool and quiet. Perfect for running.

Jay had a plan. He couldn't change the fact that he was thirteen, almost fourteen, and very likely the youngest player at basketball camp. He couldn't change the fact that, even at five-seven, he was below the average height. He couldn't change the fact that he was on Chad's Tornadoes, waiting for a bad weather report. But, there was something he might possibly change. If he ran laps every morning before anyone else was up, he might buildup enough stamina and speed so that he could at least keep up with the rest of the guys or, with a lot of luck, be chosen to play in the weekend tournament. He was starting to get two letters of the alphabet under control: M and E. Now, all he had to do was focus on P.

He walked down the hill to the town's main street. There were only few cars on the move, maybe people ending a night shift or finally getting home after a party that wouldn't quit. He crossed the gymnasium lawn and walked to the track that circled around the football field.

Cool dampness filled his lungs as he breathed in deeply and reached his hands high above his head. He bent to touch the toes of his new white-and-blue sneakers. Then he lunged into long stretches. He flexed his feet to feel the pull along the backs of his legs.

Jay looked at the dirt track curving ahead of him, took a determined breath, and started to jog. He didn't notice that he had company. Someone else had walked down the hill that morning, not long before Jay had. That person was sitting in the shadows of the stadium bleachers, seventh row. He was watching as Jay started his first lap.

* * *

Mike's bed was empty when Jay got back from the track. His towel wasn't on the hook, so Jay figured he must be in the shower. Good. He didn't want anyone asking questions about where he'd been and why he was dripping with sweat. Later, if Mike asked where he was, he'd just say he'd been watching cartoons on TV. That made sense. Sort of.

He peeled off his shorts and old T-shirt and threw them on the floor of his closet, then headed down the hall to the showers.

Chad was shaving at one of the sinks, careful not to eliminate that small patch under his lip. He was talking to another junior coach through the thick foam around his mouth, waving the plastic razor for emphasis in case anyone hadn't noticed he was shaving.

"Hey," said Mike. "Where'd you disappear to?"

"TV lounge. Just watching cartoons."

"Like all the other little kiddies early in the morning, eh?" Chad's pink-and-yellow grin smeared through the white shaving foam.

Jay stepped under the shower nozzle and let the stream of hot water drown out any other sarcastic remarks Chad might come up with.

The Tornadoes were in their last eight minutes of a game against the Sharks with the score sitting at 14–14. The other teams sat in the bleachers, cheering the good plays and making mental note of mistakes they'd avoid when it was their turn to play basketball.

Martin was the player to watch. His eyes never left the ball; his large hands were always anticipating a pass; he made speed look effortless. He was a team player, never hogging the ball and always quick to reassure a guy who'd fumbled or to recognize a guy who'd executed a perfect play.

Jay had lots of opportunity to watch Martin. Throughout this practice game, Jay had been warming the bench. Again. His Basketball Nova Scotia T-shirt didn't even have the first stains of sweat. He was getting the distinct feeling that his coach had forgotten there was a sixth player waiting to get onto the basketball court.

With all this bench time, Jay got a good look at Chad's coaching skills, especially the skills he didn't have. The only time he shouted to his guys was to remind them of what they were doing wrong: "watch the ball," or "get the lead out," or "smarten up." He never shouted any encouragement. Also, Chad muttered a lot. When he got heated up (which was often), his vocabulary deteriorated into four-letter words. "Nice" wasn't one of them. If a referee made a call that he didn't agree with, he'd jump up in frustration, practically spitting out one of those four-letter words from under his breath. Chad the coach was a lot like Chad the driver: quick-tempered and pushy.

Suddenly, the basketball battle between the Tornadoes and the Sharks heated up. A Shark fumbled the ball and a Tornado took possession. Jay watched the wave of players reverse direction. Martin was open for a long pass. He received it and dribbled swiftly over the center line toward the Sharks' basket. Two guards moved in fast to trap him, but he made a slick bounce pass out of the tangle. The Tornado forward accepted Martin's pass, pivoted, focused, and went up for an easy two points. Swish, and the net danced.

Jay put his little fingers between his lips and gave a piercing whistle. "Way t'go, Tornadoes!"

The Sharks' coach called for a time out.

Chad pulled his players into a huddle, telling them not to lose their cool now that they had this narrow lead. Jay got up off the bench and joined the huddle. What happened next, he hadn't expected at all.

"I gotta sit out the rest of the game." Martin was leaning over, both palms against his knees. Then, he bent his right leg slowly a couple of times.

"What're you talking about?"

"Somethin' doesn't feel right. It's my knee. Maybe somethin' happened on that last play."

"Nothing happened on that last play. I saw every second of it. You're fine."

"Jay can sub in."

"Oh, so now you're the coach? Listen up, Martin. I say who plays and who doesn't. And I'm saying you play."

Everyone in the huddle felt the tension between coach and player. Seconds ticked away. Martin walked over to the Tornadoes' bench, slightly favouring his right leg. He sat down.

The whistle blew, ending the time out.

"Get your players into position, coach!" shouted the referee.

Chad had no choice. "Jay, you're in."

A hint of a smile snuck across Martin's face. That's when

Jay realized what had just happened. Martin didn't have an injury. He was faking it, forcing Chad to put Jay in the game. Why? What's it to Martin?

The Sharks were hyped, anxious to swallow the two-point lead the Tornadoes had gained. The action shifted into overdrive. Jay's basketball instincts kicked in immediately. A Shark was moving the ball up the court and got into position to score. Jay saw the line the ball would take even before it left the Shark's hands. He jumped and blocked successfully.

The Tornadoes were in control. But not for long. Two guards raced to obstruct the Tornado forward. One of them smacked the ball out of his grip and the other Shark grabbed it. Jay made himself into a roadblock in front of his opponent. The forward halted, pivoted right, and pivoted left. He was trapped, holding the basketball above his head. Jay tipped it to a Tornado who was clear for a breakaway. Before the Sharks had time to set up their defense, the Tornadoes' score had jumped ahead by two more points.

Jay's adrenaline was pumping. His lungs stung from exertion and his cheeks burned red. For the past couple of minutes, though, he hadn't been thinking about being younger or shorter or slower. He was just thinking about being on a winning team.

When the Sharks and the Tornadoes shook hands and left the floor, two other teams got into position on the basketball court. Martin joined his team in the bleachers, hardly favouring his right leg at all now.

"Seems like you got a miracle cure on that leg," said Chad.

"Yeah. Something like that," said Martin. He let Chad's sarcastic tone slide off him like rain off a roof.

"I know what you did," said Jay, sitting next to Martin. "Thanks."

"I didn't do nothin'."

"I mean, Chad wouldn't have played me. The score was too close."

"You're here to play basketball. Am I right?"

"Yeah, but—"

"So you can't play basketball when your butt is warmin' the bench."

"I'm not fast like guys here."

"So? You're already doing something about that."

"What do you mean?"

"Runnin' at the track."

"How— "

"I saw you."

"Huh?"

"This morning. I was in the bleachers."

"Oh." Weird, thought Jay. How come a guy would be up so early just sitting alone like that? But he kept his questions to himself. Not that he figured Martin would've answered them anyway.

"I got this idea to run laps. Build up on my running. It's probably useless."

"You just need to know what to do."

"Yeah. Or maybe I should wait till my legs get longer."

Jay had a sudden image of Sam. He could see the little guy standing against the wall in the kitchen where they were both measured on their birthdays. Sam would try to be as tall as he possibly could, stretching his neck up and holding his breath. When the pencil mark was made and the date written beside it, he'd step back and admire his achievement of growing taller every year.

But Jay didn't have years to wait. Was he going to end his basketball career at the age of thirteen, almost fourteen, just because his legs were shorter than these giants at basketball camp?

* * *

It was about an hour before the dining hall would open to the regular lineup of empty stomachs. Jay was alone in his dorm room. Because his window was wide open, he could hear every word people were saying down in the parking lot. A guy laughed and called someone a loser, though it didn't sound like he meant it. Then a girl shouted, "You going to Jeff's party?" and another girl yelled back, "Don't know! Call me later!"

That's when Jay thought about calling home. He went to the pay phone near the TV lounge and dialed Gramp's number.

"Hello. This is Sam."

"I'd like to speak with Rudy, if he's available," said Jay with a smirk on his face.

Sam giggled, then shouted, "Rudy! Here boy! Someone called you up. I think it's the dog catcher."

The phone clunked against Rudy's chain collar and Jay could hear the dog panting. Sam was still giggling in the background.

"Hey, Rudy! How's it goin'? Good boy. Good dog." Jay looked around to make sure no one was listening in on this ridiculous telephone conversation. "Sam? Okay, Sam. Rudy gets the idea. Sam? Sam!"

"We're going swimming. At the beach. But not Dad. And not Gramp. Just me and Mom and Rudy."

"Cool, Sam. That'll be fun. Make sure you put your water wings on if the waves are big."

"Will you be home?"

"Yeah, but not today."

"Tomorrow?"

"Next week."

"You could swim, too."

"Yeah, but not today. Next week, when I come home. Okay?"

"Okay."

"Can I talk to Mom, Sam?"

"Mom!" shouted Sam. "Jay's in the phone!"

"On the phone," corrected Jay. But Sam wasn't listening anymore.

"Hello dear. Is everything all right?"

"Sure Mom. Just thought I'd call. Let you know how basketball camp's going."

"And how is it going?"

"Oh, pretty good." As soon as he started talking, Jay knew he wasn't going to blab on and on about being too short and too young and not fast enough and not included in the games enough. "Everyone got these cool T-shirts that have, like, waves with a sailboat and with a basketball that looks like the sun. Our team's called the Tornadoes. It's way different from being at school. Some of these guys are just about pros. Mike's brother's my coach."

"We miss you. I'm glad you're enjoying yourself."

"Me too, Mom." Jay knew he was really talking about missing everyone and not actually about enjoying himself.

"Sam and I are just getting ready to go to the beach to cool off a bit before supper. Sam's standing here in his bathing suit." Her voice trailed away from the receiver. "Get your surf socks, sweetheart. And take those water wings off Rudy. No, he'll be fine. Yes, he can swim in big waves. I'm glad you called us, Jay. I'll tell Dad. Is there anything else, dear?"

Mike was coming down the hall now, and Chad was with him.

"Ah, no, Mom. Just checking in," said Jay quietly.

"We love you, Jay."

"Me too, Mom. Bye."

He hung up the phone and smiled at Mike and Chad.

"You guys up to anything tonight?" asked Chad.

"Probably watch TV," said Jay. "Maybe some basketball videos."

"I'm gonna be partying. Someone's birthday. Friend of a friend of a friend. Who cares?" He smirked like he had already had too much beer.

* * *

Seven hours later, Chad had definitely had too much beer. Jay was sound asleep when Mike woke him up.

"Jay. You gotta help me get Chad. I think he passed out."

Jay wiped his eyes and tried to clear his foggy brain. What was happening? Where was he? He looked at the clock. 1:09.

Mike was standing at the window. "He's not moving."

Jay got out of bed to take a look. In the shadows from the parking lot light, he could see a lump of a person lying beside a bush.

He hauled on his jeans and a T-shirt, and quickly followed Mike down the stairs and outside.

Chad lifted his cheek off the ground and grinned stupidly at them. They pulled him to his feet and forced him to move one foot in front of the other. Going up the stairs was a struggle, like trying to manoeuvre a large duffle bag full of wet towels. Burps of Chad's beer breath just about suffocated them. As they coaxed him along the hall toward his room, the burps got a bit more complicated.

"Uh-oh," said Chad.

"Quick," said Mike. "The bathroom. Fast."

Jay just about lost his own cookies, listening to the splash of vomit in the toilet bowl and smelling the stench of beer and remnants of fried food. Chad was on his knees, supporting his head on one arm. Mike was holding his brother's forehead and trying not to watch the action in the toilet bowl.

Jay had to step away from the cubicle. "He can't have much left to chuck," he said drearily.

"Get me some paper towels. Wet ones."

Jay handed the paper towels to Mike. He could see that Mike was just as grossed out as he was, but he was doing what he had to do. It was his brother. What choice did he have?

The washroom door opened and Martin walked in. "'Sup?"

"Uh …" Mike was scrambling for a lie to cover their tracks.

"That Chad?"

"He was at a party," said Jay.

"Some party," said Martin and stepped up to a urinal.

"Listen," said Mike. "If anyone finds out—"

"This means nothin' to me," said Martin. "I've got no reason to tell anyone. If your big brother wants to fill up his guts with booze and deposit it all in a toilet, that's his business."

Eventually, Chad did stop upchucking and Mike stopped flushing the toilet.

They got Chad into his room, where his roommate was snoring heavily, his face turned to the wall. "Hope he doesn't wake up," whispered Mike.

"If he does, it won't take him long to figure things out anyway."

In the dim light spilling in from the hall, they stripped off Chad's soiled T-shirt and flopped him onto the bed.

"What should I do with this T-shirt?" asked Mike.

"Throw it in the garbage. It stinks."

They gently closed the door and went back to their room.

"Guess he'll have a big head when he wakes up."

"Yeah, but he'll be okay. We better catch some sleep." Jay turned off the light and curled into his own bed, trying to get images of Chad and splashes of vomit and fumes of beer out of his mind.

"I really appreciate what you did," said Mike.

"No problem."

"You think anyone'll find out? He might get in trouble."

"No one'll find out."

"What about Martin? What if he says something?"

"He won't. He hardly ever talks anyway."

The dark room was quiet for a few minutes. Then Mike said, "I never saw Chad drunk before." His voice sounded fragile.

Jay knew Mike looked up to his older brother. Chad was some kind of hero to him, playing basketball for Acadia University and now learning to be a coach. It must be tough to look down at the guy you look up to, especially when he's chucking his guts out into a toilet.

What could Jay say that would be any help to Mike right now? Nothing. He pretended he had already fallen asleep.

4

A New Coach

Jay built a mental block around his list of *Things to feel weird about at basketball camp* and started making a new list: *Ways to survive basketball camp*. Number one on the list was *Stop thinking about being too young and too short and too slow*. Number two on the list was: *Find a running coach*.

If his hunch was right, he would find a running coach that morning, before birds even had time to wake up. Today he would do some serious running. His new Basketball Nova Scotia T-shirt was about to get soaked with streams of sweat.

Jay walked down the campus hill and went straight to the bleachers. Just as he thought, there was Martin sitting by himself about six rows up.

"I've got a favour to ask," said Jay without sitting down. "I mean, it's up to you if you do it or not, but—"

"Do what?"

"I need you to coach me."

"What're you talkin' about?"

"I'm talking about running. I don't have time to wait till my legs get longer. You said I just need to know what to do."

"Why me?"

"You're the best runner. And it doesn't look like you mind

getting up early in the morning."

Martin leaned forward, his elbows on his knees and the fingers of his hands locked together. Then he leaned back, rubbed one hand across his cheek and scratched the small circle of fuzz on his chin. His bottom lip disappeared under his top lip. Finally, he looked up at Jay. "You serious about this?"

"Sure I'm serious."

"Okay then. I'm your coach." He raised his palm and Jay slapped a high five to seal the deal.

Together they walked down from the bleachers and onto the track.

"It's fifty percent skill and one hundred percent attitude," said Martin. His usual don't-get-in-my-face look had suddenly changed. It was like he wasn't even the same guy anymore. He was Martin, the coach; and he obviously took this job very seriously. "A runner's got to know he's gonna be fast. He's got to see his speed in his own mind like some kind of powerful animal. He's got to keep his eyes on where he's gonna be, not where he is at the moment. See the future, just a few seconds up ahead."

Even if Martin's math didn't add up and his words only partly painted the picture, Jay had a definite feeling this plan was going to work. He just might survive basketball camp.

"Now, the first thing you've got to think about is your head. Hold it up. Face forward. Right. Now think about how your head is on top of your spine. You don't want your spine all curved-like. A spine is supposed to be straight. It holds you up. There. Not too stiff. Just straight. That's it."

Jay concentrated on every instruction.

"I don't want speed right now. Just go for posture."

As Jay started a slow jog, Martin kept pace with him, running along, studying each move, coaching him through one full lap.

Next, Martin taught Jay how to set his own running rhythm

by listening to his heart, to his breath going in and out, and to his footfalls on the track. But when Jay concentrated on rhythm, he forgot everything he'd just learned about posture.

"Where are your eyes? Where are your shoulders?" Martin kept running beside Jay, never raising his voice. "That's good. Okay, now, breathe loud. Air in. Air out. Match it to your pace. Left, right. Left, right. Air in, air out. There. You got it. Oh. Lost it. Try again. Where are your eyes?"

* * *

When basketball drills began later that morning, Jay felt slightly more confident. He kept Martin's instructions in his mind: *Don't lean into the run. Square your shoulders. Keep your elbows bent, hands up. Breathe. Get your rhythm. Don't watch your sneakers. Chin up. Eyes straight ahead. Set your goal.*

Chad was acting very different, and it wasn't because of all the beer he'd consumed last night. He probably didn't remember much about that anyway. Today was Chad's turn to be supervised by Jamie, the assistant coach, and he was doing everything he could to make the best impression. He turned down the volume on his voice and dropped the sarcasm. He picked some new terms out of his coaches' handbook and threw them around every chance he got: "Play with pride," and "Now, *that's* basketball," and "Team cohesion wins the game!"

Chad called his Tornadoes into a huddle when the drills ended and the first competition game was ready to begin. The Tornadoes would play against the Panthers. This meant that Jay would be Mike's opponent, which felt familiar, just like last year when Jay still played for the Richmond Rockets and Mike held down the centre position with the Centreville Cougars.

"Okay, guys, listen up," said Chad. "The Panthers know

what they're up against. You guys've shown strong team identity, just about flawless ball handling, and you're masters under that basket. You know how to support each other. You know how to push our score into the high double digits. The Tornadoes will triumph! Let's hear it!"

"Gooooo, TORNADOES!!"

"Okay. Starters are: Steve, Chris, Martin, Brent, and Jay. Let's go!"

Jamie made a few pencil marks about Chad's performance in his small notebook. Jay figured he was writing something like: *Supports his players. Builds team spirit. Even plays shortest guy in first quarter.*

"Keep an eye out for me," said Martin, giving Jay a pat on the back as they jogged onto the court.

Martin, at centre, controlled the jump and tipped the ball to Brent. Jay moved toward the Panthers' basket, keeping Martin in view. The action reversed suddenly when a Panther stole the ball mid-bounce right out from under Brent's palm. A long pass went to Mike, who wasted no time crossing the centreline. He slowed the pace until his team got into position.

Jay's breath was already broken into short gasps. He forced himself to forget about that and concentrate on where he was and what would happen next.

Steve made a wall in front of Mike, but Mike slipped a bounce pass under his arms. A Panther beneath the basket now had the ball. But he didn't go up for the dunk. He forced the Tornadoes to focus on him for half a second and made a quick pass back to Mike, who was now free. Mike leaped and sent the basketball in a strong, sure arc through the hoop. Swish!

Panthers 2. Tornadoes 0.

Chad called for a substitution and sent Ronny in for Steve. Jay only had time for a quick glance at the bench. Chad patted Steve's shoulder as if to say *Don't worry about it*. Sure, thought Jay. Don't worry about it as long as Jamie's here making those supervision notes.

Ronny took the ball out of bounds, looking for a way in. Jay saw the chance for a pick-and-roll, which freed Martin for the pass. Two guards moved in fast to slow Martin's progress, but Martin zigzagged around the obstacles and invaded Panther territory. He passed back to Brent, who fumbled. The ball went wild and a Panther grabbed it. Jay rushed to block the pass just as it left the Panther's hands. Out of the corner of his eye, he saw that Martin was free. He tipped the ball to Martin, who went up for a two-point slam dunk.

From the bench, Chad shouted, "Now, *that's* basketball!"

But when the Tornadoes came off the floor at the end of the game, their score wasn't on top. The Panthers had grabbed the victory with a final score of 52–48. Chad's frown was carved in stone.

Although Jay had burned up all his energy and his team had lost, he still felt pretty good. Out there on the floor, Martin had given him a couple of reassuring nods. And nothing was sweeter than that tip he had made to Martin, followed by that swift slam dunk.

"Coach, call your players together," said Jamie. He still had his pencil and notepad in his hands.

In the huddle, Chad seemed to forget all the positive reinforcement stuff he might've read in his coaches' handbook. "Better luck next time, guys. The Panthers have some top players to keep down. Like my brother. Mike's a guy to look out for." Then he must have seen some disapproval in Jamie's eyes. "So let's take a bit of a break here. Cool down. Think back on this game and be proud you kept the score close. Some nice plays, guys. Really."

Jay imagined Jamie's supervision notes: *Coaches best when winning. Could improve on sincerity skills. Needs to build on people skills.*

* * *

Jay finished the last long stretch, reaching forward to touch his toes. Martin had just said he already saw an improvement in Jay's running, even though this was only the second day of coaching. That was a big plus.

They were getting along really great, here on the track and on the basketball court, too. Martin didn't say much, but Jay was thinking he probably felt the same way. They were friends.

"I think I know the reason you don't like it if anyone calls you Marty," said Jay. He was sitting on the grass, leaning back on one elbow.

Martin reached forward, touching one foot and then the other. He held the stretch with his head on his knees. Then he sat up. "What got you thinkin' about that?"

"I dunno. But I remember what you said to Chad the other day. *Martin. No 'y'.*"

"So what's the reason?"

"You're named after Martin Luther King. No one would call him Marty."

Martin hauled off his T-shirt and used it as a towel to wipe the sweat from his forehead and chest. "My birthday's January 15th. Same as Martin Luther King's. Dad named me."

"I saw your Dad, if that was him who drove you here. I was looking out the window."

"Yeah, that was him." There wasn't any enthusiasm in Martin's voice.

It made Jay remember a small detail about that first day.

When Martin got out of the van, he had walked away without looking back, or waving goodbye, or saying anything. He just shut the door and left. Didn't much look like this father and son were a winning team.

Jay decided to keep any other personal questions to himself. If he and Martin were friends right now, he didn't want to mess that up.

Martin stood and offered Jay a hand. Then he grinned. "I heard you talkin' on the phone to your dog."

"Wha— I didn't know anyone was listening." His face burned red.

"I was in the TV room."

"Sam, he's my little brother. Well, he answered the phone, and I pretended I wanted to talk to Rudy. The crazy kid put the dog on the phone."

"So what'd Rudy have to say?"

Jay cracked a smile, and Martin gave him a punch in the shoulder.

* * *

Mike had not gone for breakfast yet when Jay returned to their room. He looked upset.

"What's up?"

"I don't know where Chad is," said Mike. "His roommate said he didn't come back last night. And his car's not in the parking lot."

"It's no big deal. Maybe he's met some girl or something." Jay could see that Mike wasn't reassured. "What do you wanna do?"

"I don't know."

"We could tell someone he's missing."

"What if we get him into trouble?"

"Let's catch breakfast after I grab a shower. Then we can check his room again."

"Sure. Right. Maybe he'll be back by then." Mike's shoulders drooped with worry.

After breakfast, Chad's bed was still empty. They asked around, but even the other junior coaches didn't know where he might have gone. Most of them said he'd be back by practice.

But he wasn't.

All the players sat on the gym floor in front of the flip chart. Jamie instructed them on a few team strategies, including inbound plays and man-to-man defence. His blue marker made broad swoops across the page, creating a snarled map that only a basketball mind could follow.

Mike watched the door to the gym more than carefully than he watched Jamie's blue marker. Jay found it hard to concentrate, too.

Jamie flipped the chart paper over and switched his instruction to individual technical skills. One-on-one. Two-on-two. Three-on-three.

Out of the corner of his eye, Jay saw Chad peering into the gym from the doorway, trying to keep out of sight. Smart. No sense drawing everyone's attention to the fact that he was arriving very late for practice.

Jay gently elbowed Mike and nodded in the direction of the door.

"Something's wrong," Mike whispered when he saw Chad.

Jamie finished his instructions and told the teams to meet with their coaches. When Jay got close to Chad, he could see that Mike had been right about something being wrong. Chad's lower lip was swollen and split, just above that small patch of facial hair.

Jamie hadn't been fooled by Chad's attempt to blend in with the crowd. "Mr. Murphy," he said, walking toward the Tornadoes.

"You are late. I hope there's an explanation." When he saw the lip, his tone changed to concern. "Let me see that." He held Chad's chin up to get a closer look. "How'd that happen?"

"I fell."

"Fell." Jamie let go of Chad's chin. "It doesn't need stitches, but we'll get some ointment on that before you begin working with your team. Come with me." He turned toward the Tornadoes. "Guys, try a few of those drills we just went over. Divide yourselves up for two-on-two."

Jay saw Mike watching from across the gym as Jamie and Chad made their way to the coach's small office. The door closed behind them.

The Tornadoes still hadn't moved.

"What happened to him?"

"He didn't fall, that's for sure."

"Fell on someone's fist."

"We gonna play basketball or what?" Martin picked up a ball. "Jay you're with me against Steve and Chris. Let's go."

It was at least six minutes before the coach's door opened and Chad came back out. His lower lip was painted white with ointment. Maybe that was the reason he wasn't smiling.

When the morning clinic was almost over, the head coach called all the players and the junior coaches together again.

"Okay, guys, listen up. Friday's the day. I don't need to tell you that. Jamie and I and your team coaches have begun making notes and talking about which of you will play in this weekend's invitational tournament. Six guys will wear varsity uniforms: two for Acadia, two for Dalhousie, and two for Saint Mary's. Today's Wednesday. Friday we post the names. You've still got time to show us your best."

Jay thought about how cool it would be playing for a university team and wearing a varsity basketball jersey. *There's the*

basketball sailing toward him. A long pass. He's open under the
basket. His guard scrambles into position. Too late. Jay receives
the ball and leaps. Swish! Two points! The crowd goes wild!

"Selecting six players isn't going to be an easy job. There's lots of talent in this gymnasium. Lots of talent." The coach looked slowly around, making eye contact with the players sitting on the floor. Jay was pretty sure the coach's eyes had slid blindly past him and landed on Martin.

Jay made his own varsity picks: Martin, for pure talent and keeping his cool; Mike, for height and for high scoring; maybe Steve for showing promise. He left his own name off the list.

In the dining hall, Jay noticed Mike having lunch with Chad. Maybe Mike was getting a few details about Chad's disappearing act and his cut lip.

About half an hour later, back in the gym, Mike filled Jay in on some of those details.

"Chad says he found this great place to swim. There's this deserted mill on some back road somewhere."

"Yeah?"

"Yeah. That's where he was last night. He went with a bunch of people he knows. There's this wall where you jump off into this deep pond. He said it was so dark you hardly see the water. Just splashes where other people jumped."

"Weird."

"Yeah. That's how he cut his lip. Jumped too close to another guy. Hit the guy right in the knee."

"Ooh, bet that hurt." Jay tried to picture the scenario: nighttime, deserted mill, dark pond, people jumping off a wall, people splashing in the water. Who knows? Maybe Chad actually did jump off that wall and smash into some guy's knee. It could have happened. Mike definitely believed it could have happened.

"He says he'll take me there. You could come, too."

"Yeah? When?"

"Maybe tomorrow night."

"Tomorrow?"

Jay wasn't exactly jumping at the offer, and Mike picked up on it. "You don't want to go because of Chad. I can tell. You think he'll be drinking or something. Get us into trouble."

"I ... ah…" Talking in Morse code wasn't helping the things.

"Chad's not always like that, ya know." Mike looked almost angry. "And besides, he's nineteen. It's not like it's against the law to party."

"I didn't say Chad would get us into trouble."

"You're too serious. Lighten up. Have some fun for a change."

Jamie came out of his office carrying a flip chart and set it up near centre court. "Find a spot over here, everyone. Let's review a couple of plays."

Mike's comments had jabbed at Jay's pride. Was he really too serious? Somehow, Mike had mentally erased how uptight he had been when Chad drank too much and when he had disappeared. Maybe that was the trick. Instead of being serious, just whitewash everything in your brain until you have nothing to be uptight about.

He sat on the floor next to Mike. "I'll go swimming," he said. "Sounds fun."

But the whitewashing job wasn't quite working. How much fun could it be swimming in the dark at some deserted mill where who knows what kind of danger was ready to creep out of the darkness or float up from the depths?

5

Double Depression

Jamie recapped his blue marker and folded the flip chart. "So remember. A player with the ball may be double-teamed by the opposition, but a team may not double-team a player who does not have possession of the ball. Everyone clear on that? Coaches, take your players through a few drills."

The Tornadoes gathered around Chad. No one mentioned his fat lip and the white ointment still smeared over the cut. "Let's have a look at the double-team rule and see what you can do with it," said Chad. "Jay, you've got the ball. Martin and Steve, you guys want to stop him. Ronny, you get ready for a pass from Jay. Okay, let's go. "

Jay started a slow dribble. Martin and Steve moved in to double-team him. In a surprise spurt of energy, he pivoted and avoided the guards' towering arms in a slick crossover move. His pass to Ronny was just as quick.

Chad blew his whistle. A bit of the ointment stuck to the end of it.

"What're you guys doing? Waitin' for a bus?" He ignored Ronny and Jay and walked over to Martin and Steve. "You lost your opponent. How'd that happen? Don't bother telling me. We all saw what happened. You weren't ready. Let's get two more guys out here and see if we can get this right. Jay, you've still got the ball."

Martin wasn't letting Chad's tirade get to him, but Steve's face was red as a beet and his shoulders slumped.

"Nice play," said Martin as he walked back to the bench. "Fast."

Jay smiled at the compliment. He had protected the ball against two bigger, stronger players. Amazing.

The Tornadoes went through the drill a couple of times before Jamie called all the teams together. "This is your third afternoon at this basketball camp. You've had instruction, drills, scrimmages, and a couple of mini-games. You've had time to get to know your coaches and the other guys on your teams. This afternoon we're ready to play our first full-length game. Coaches, come to centre court for the draw."

"I hope we get picked," said Jay. "My game's good today. Not like Chad noticed. He only sees stuff to criticize."

"He's gotta make everyone sharp. That's his job," said Martin. "He's coachin' to win."

"Yelling and being sarcastic isn't what wins basketball games."

Jamie held up a cap with the team names inside. The first name drawn was Ravens. He put his hand back into the hat and drew the next team. "Ravens, your opponents this afternoon will be … the Tornadoes!"

Chad grabbed the stack of orange pinnies and the Ravens' coach took the blue ones. All the other players found places to sit in the bleachers while the two challengers took over the benches on opposite sides of the gymnasium. Jay tied on his pinnie. Number 17—the same number he had worn when he played those games for Centreville last season. That might be lucky … and it might not.

"Okay, guys. Listen up. If we win this first game, we've got a chance for Friday's playoff. We need the win and we need a high score. It's not just for camp medals. It's the spinoffs. Who do you think'll be picked for the varsity tournament this weekend, the losers? Who do you think recruiters'll want? Your future's tied up in this game. Think about it."

Jay's confidence was shrinking into a small grey ball of doubt. Some pep talk. It was more like a threat.

"First line: Martin, Steve, Ronny, Brent, aaaand … okay, Jay you start, too."

The Ravens had just jogged onto the floor like pros, each player dribbling a basketball. They formed a circle at the key, bouncing almost in rhythm with each other, now in front and now just behind their legs.

"You guys just gonna stand there mesmerized?" shouted Chad. "Get started on your layups."

Martin, Jay, and Ronny wove a figure eight toward the hoop, with Martin catching the final pass. Up and in! His hands easily brushed the rim of the basket in his follow-through.

Jay's first layup it hit the backboard and bounced off.

"Use the backboard," said Martin. "Don't abuse it. Go easy."

His second try didn't even touch the backboard. It rolled precariously around the rim and fell lazily through the hoop. Luck.

"Like I said, use the backboard."

The whistle blew. The Ravens and the Tornadoes jogged to their team benches. Jay got ready for another I'm-warning-you speech from Chad.

"Remember, this isn't just a game. It's your future. Play like your life depends on it. Martin, you're at centre. Brent, you're on the bench. The rest of you know your positions. Let's go."

Martin, wearing the Tornado orange, shook hands with the blue Raven. His six-foot-two height and his long arms put him a couple of inches closer to the ball than his opponent. He won the toss, easily tipping the ball to Steve.

Ronny lost his guard and raced down the outside lane. He caught Steve's pass, but got blocked in a double-team defensive press. The Ravens didn't give him an inch.

"Behind you!" shouted Martin.

Steve tossed the ball back to Martin. Jay ran into Raven territory with his guard sticking to him like glue. His sudden stop faked out the guard. Martin's pass was rapid. Now Jay had the ball. *Use the backboard.* He measured the ball's speed and angle as he jumped. Perfect precision! The basketball tipped the backboard and swished through the hoop. The net danced.

Tornadoes 2. Ravens 0.

Jay took high-fives and slaps on the back from the rest of his teammates. He hadn't made that play alone, but he could definitely take credit for completing the chain of moves with his perfect two-point layup.

The Ravens had the ball and were even more eager to score. Martin blocked a pass but tipped the ball out of bounds. The ref's whistle blew.

A Raven forward caught the long inbound pass. Steve and Ronny double-teamed him. When the Raven held the ball above his head, looking for someone in blue, Ronny slapped it free.

A scramble of orange and blue covered the ball until a Raven came out of the tangle with possession. He slowed the game down, one arm held out defensively, giving his team an opportunity to find their positions.

Martin was in sync with every move the forward made. e Tornadoes secured their positions between the ball and the Ravens. Martin's rival still controlled the play, making his way steadily toward his goal.

In a sudden break, the Raven executed a crossover and bolted past Martin, zigzagging toward the key. Martin recovered and darted in front of the forward, matching his jump and slamming the ball off its trajectory. The Raven did a sidestep and grabbed his forearm as if he'd been hit.

The ref's whistle blew. "Foul! Tornadoes. Number fourteen!"

For a split second, Martin's face showed disbelief. Then his expression washed to neutral.

"That was clean!" screamed Chad from the bench. "Gimme a break! The guy's fakin' it! He wasn't hit!"

Jay ran behind Martin and gave him a light tag on the arm. Chad was right—the play had been clean.

The teams lined up as the Raven took his first foul shot. In. One point. He shook his forearm as if to relieve an ache. Martin stayed cool.

Now both teams got ready for the rebound.

The Raven bounced the ball twice. Then he held it just above his forehead, balanced on his palm. He focused. All the other players remained alert.

Up and in! Ravens 2. Tornadoes 2.

Steve took the ball out of bounds. The pass went to Ronny but hit the tips of his fingers and was grabbed by a Raven.

The game moved back into the court under the Tornadoes' basket and the Raven looked around to make a pass.

Jay tagged his forward, making a wall between him and the basketball. The wall was too close. The forward, when he caught the pass, tripped over Jay's sneaker and they both fell.

"Foul, Tornadoes seventeen."

"Slow things down!" yelled Chad from the bench. "Control that ball!"

Jay was a bit shaken from the spill. His right wrist felt like something had disconnected. He tried to cover it up so Chad wouldn't pull him out of the game.

The inbound pass went to a Raven near centre court. With sure control, the six-footer dribbled the ball swiftly down the outside lane beyond the reach of the Tornado guards. He chanced a long shot. The ball curved up, then completed the semicircle with a perfect glide in through the basket.

Ravens 4. Tornadoes 2.

Martin took the ball out of bounds under the basket, leaving little time for the Ravens to cheer about their lead. His quick bounce pass caught Jay off guard and he fumbled. A Raven grabbed the lose ball and leaped up for a slam dunk.

Ravens 6. Tornadoes 2.

Chad signalled madly for a time out.

"Uh-oh," said Jay as he jogged beside Martin back to the Tornadoes' bench.

"That was my fault, not yours. I should've slowed the action."

"I should've been ready." Jay's wrist still stung.

"So, what's with you guys? Eh? What're you thinking out there? I know the answer to that. You're not thinking anything. Blank. Zip. Zilch." Chad wiped his hand absently across his mouth, taking all the white ointment off in one swoop. He looked down at his hand as if he didn't know where the smudge of white had come from. "Martin, take a seat. Brent, you're in. I don't believe you guys. It's like you didn't hear a word I said. I'm telling you, if we lose this game, there's gonna be—"

Chad's tirade was cut off by the referee's whistle.

Jay swallowed a few gulps of water before running onto the 'urt. He gently rubbed his wrist. Some ice would sure feel ` on it.

Martin sat down on the bench, his elbows on his knees, ready to study the game.

Chad rubbed his hands together to absorb the smeared ointment.

Brent lost the toss and the Ravens sped smoothly down the floor as if pulled by magnets. Again they fed the ball to the tallest Raven. He jumped and scored.

Ravens 8. Tornadoes 2.

At the end of the first half, the Ravens had a four-point lead.

Jay was hoping for some bench time in the second half. His wrist was throbbing now. Maybe he'd sprained it. His lungs were stinging from the exertion of running from one end of that long gymnasium to the other, trying to keep up with the Ravens' speed.

"Let's just hand the ball over to these guys and call it quits," said Chad. "Because it looks like that's what you want. You're not playing with determination. You're not playing with guts."

"I could use some ice," said Jay. "My wrist might be sprained."

"Oh, now we gotta hear excuses."

"If the guy needs ice, he needs ice," said Martin.

"Let me see that wrist."

Jay cautiously showed it to Chad. "It only hurts a little."

"You saying you can't play?"

"Maybe it'll be okay after I get some ice on it."

"Jay's on the bench. Martin, you play centre. Brent, move into Jay's position." Chad looked around at his team as if they were basketball camp dropouts. "I want that four-point gap gone. Fast." Then he added as an afterthought, "Jay, get some ice if you really need it. Ice packs are in Jamie's office."

Jay came back to the bench, holding the ice pack against his wrist. The cold was doing its magic. Maybe it would numb the ache long enough for him to get back into the action of the game.

The Tornadoes kicked into overdrive. They were now unstoppable. In minutes, the Ravens' four-point lead disappeared and the Tornadoes pushed ahead by two. Then four. Then six.

From where Jay sat, he'd have to say Martin was the main reason for the Tornadoes' turnaround. The plays had Martin's fingerprints all over them. And he scored just about half the points. In a couple of long shots he sent the ball in an easy arc, like a rainbow with a pot of gold at the other end. Points piled up and sparkled on the Tornadoes' side of the scoreboard.

At the three-quarter point, Chad's mood had definitely changed. "You've got them all nerved up. They're fumbling out there like amateurs."

Jay put the ice pack aside, anxious to get back into the game. "My wrist's okay now. I can play."

"Let's not change the lineup. Might change our luck."

When the whistle blew to end the break, Jay was still sharing the bench with Chad.

The Ravens were left with no high branches to perch on after the Tornadoes stormed through. The final score was 51–38.

Chad acted like he had just won the lottery. Jay heard him say something to the Ravens' coach about how dangerous it was getting caught in the path of the Tornadoes.

Before he left the floor, the Ravens' coach took a minute to say a few things to Martin. Whatever he said, it must've been pretty good because Jay saw Martin smile. A real smile.

Mike came over to the Tornadoes' bench, shaking Chad's hand and giving him a brother-to-brother slap on the back. "What a comeback in that second half! What'd you do? Promise your team a thousand bucks or what?"

"Or what," said Chad and laughed. "You gotta be tough

with these guys. That's what they respond to. Forget promises and deals."

"Whatever works works," said Mike. "Jay, what's up with your hand?"

"It's my wrist. Sprained it, I think. Feels okay now. Just needed ice."

"Too bad you missed that second half. Hey, Martin! Some ball control! You're MVP material, absolutely."

Mike couldn't have been more excited about the victory if it had been his own. Having a big brother coach a winning basketball team must be a lot better than having a big brother upchuck into a toilet or turn up with a split lip, thought Jay. Lucky Mike was out of earshot when his hero brother was giving those pep talks. Pepto-Dismal talks.

The Tornadoes cheered their triumph in the locker room. But Jay didn't feel like part of the team at all now. That first basket he'd scored was like ancient history. His foul and his fumble were now front-page news. Those two mistakes had cost the Tornadoes their early lead, and all Jay had done after that was watch from the sidelines. He was more valuable to his team sitting on the bench than playing on the basketball court.

If it was like Chad said, if the guys who would get to play in the weekend tournament would be picked from winning teams, then it sure wouldn't include players who fouled and fumbled and sprained a wrist and sat on the bench for half the game.

Now that the freezing ice pack was off his wrist, the throbbing ache returned. Jay felt miserable.

What was he doing at this basketball camp anyway? And what sense did it make getting out of bed at the crack of dawn and running around the track like it was going to make a difference? Not even a coach as good as Martin could work that kind of miracle.

Two more days of drills and games. Then two days for the weekend tournament. Then home.

Maybe he should just take it easy. Stop being so serious, like Mike said, even about basketball. Stop thinking he could compete with guys who are older, taller, and faster.

He had to do something. Otherwise the next four days would be dreary, dismal, discouraging, and depressing.

6

Police Escort

Late that night, Jay woke out of a restless sleep. Thunder rumbled far off in the distance. It wasn't long before lightning zigzagged across the sky outside his window and thunder smashed directly overhead. The clouds opened up and it poured buckets of rain. One sudden clap of thunder exploded so violently it felt as if the dorm roof was about to crash in.

"You awake?" said Mike.

"Who isn't?" said Jay. "Man, that was loud."

"No kidding."

Lightning again split the night sky and thunder rolled like a hundred empty oil barrels tumbling past.

"Rudy hates thunder," said Jay. "He just shakes like a leaf. Hope they're not getting this storm back home."

But he silently wished the bad weather would stick around the campus for a while. If it were still stormy in the morning, he wouldn't have to make excuses to Martin about why he wasn't going to the track.

* * *

A firm finger jabbed Jay's shoulder. He woke up and rolled

over, half opening his eyes.

"What's with you?" Martin stood beside Jay's bed wearing his black shorts and his red T-shirt with the sleeves cut off. He was ready for running.

"It's too stormy."

"What're you talkin' about? The sun's out. Get movin'."

"I'm not going."

"Sure you're goin'."

"No. I mean it." Jay sat up and rubbed his eyes. "I changed my mind about practising."

Martin folded his arms across his broad chest and gave Jay a long look. "I don't get it."

By now Mike was awake, too. "Can't a guy sleep around here? First that thunderstorm and now you guys: *I'm not going. You are going.* Gimme a break." He turned his face to the wall and pulled the covers over his head.

Jay got out of bed and hauled on his shorts. Martin followed him out of the room and shut the door quietly behind them.

This was exactly the moment he didn't want to face.

"So?" said Martin.

"It's not gonna work. I don't mean about you coaching me. I mean … Well, there's no way I'll ever get picked for the tournament. What's the use of even trying?"

"I thought you wanted to improve your game."

"I did, but—"

"You bought into all that crap Chad said, didn't you? Like about your basketball career being finished if you don't make this cut."

"It made sense. In a way."

"You believe what you wanna believe."

"Look, I'm five-seven. You're at least six feet."

"Six-two."

"Right. See what I mean? Everyone here's way taller than me. I'm out of my league. Why get my hopes up for nothing?"

"You're wastin' my time." Martin walked down the hall toward the stairs. Without stopping, he turned and said, "It's obvious you know nothin' about Spud Webb."

Jay went back into his room and looked out the window. He watched Martin come out of the dorm and head for the track alone. Quitting running practice maybe wasn't such a good idea. It was like quitting a new friend. A cop-out. Major depressing.

And Spud Webb? What was that all about?

* * *

Before practice started that morning, Jay went to Jamie's office and asked for an ice pack. "My wrist doesn't feel right."

"That sprain shouldn't still hurt. We gotta get it looked at. I'll take you over to Medical Services. Tell your coach you won't be playing this morning."

"It'll be okay. It just hurts a little. No big deal."

"Can't take a chance."

Instead of sitting in the bleachers pretending he needed an ice pack on his wrist, Jay sat in the doctor's waiting room pretending his wrist needed urgent medical attention. After a two-hour wait, the doctor took two seconds to make his diagnosis. He lifted and twisted and bent Jay's wrist, then he said, "Nothing a good game of basketball won't fix."

Back at the gym, Jay joined in on some layup drills and then some pick-and-roll practice. He gave as little effort as he could without sending Chad into a screaming fit. Not once did he make eye contact with Martin.

Only an hour left before lunch.

Jay carried his lunch tray to a corner of the cafeteria at the far end of a long table. Music students were at the other end of the table. Instrument cases of all colors, shapes, and sizes were on the floor next to their chairs. Jay tried to guess what was inside each case. Guitars were easy. Those long, flat cases were probably for flutes; or maybe clarinets would fit if they were taken apart. One case was shaped like a lumpy heart with a flat bottom. What the heck was in that?

It was weird thinking about how everyone at music camp got together each day to practise while everyone at basketball camp was in the gym doing the same thing, sort of. The musicians were trying to get all the notes right, and the basketball teams were trying to get all the plays right.

Jay wondered if anyone at music camp was feeling like he was right now. Like practice was useless. Like maybe this camp's not a place for amateurs. At least Jay wouldn't have an expensive instrument and a case to get rid of if this was the end of his career.

When he left the cafeteria, he knew he wasn't going back to the gym. Jamie would do another draw for teams who'd compete. The Tornadoes already played their game yesterday. Not much sense sitting on the bench all afternoon feeling depressed.

With no destination in mind, he walked across campus and then strolled along the town's main street. Under a clear blue sky, the town was hot and still. Some people were sitting at sidewalk tables outside a corner coffee shop. A few sat alone reading books while others were yakking with friends. He walked past the movie theatre where a sign said "Matinee— Wednesday and Saturday." Today was Thursday.

He stopped at a store window that featured university merchandise: hats, jackets, sweatshirts—all kinds of stuff. There were blue shorts with *Acadia* in large red letters across the bum. Maybe he'd buy a pair of those when he had some money with him. And there were kids' clothes, too. Sam might like one of those Acadia T-shirts or maybe a hat.

At the third corner, Jay turned down a quiet side street that stopped at a railroad crossing. Beyond the train tracks was a large dirt parking lot that was just about empty except for a white transfer truck delivering goods to a warehouse.

Far across the dykes and marshes he could see Cape Blomidon sticking out into the Bay of Fundy. His family had driven up there many times. They'd park at the very top of the cape and look down over the steep cliff to the valley and the bay below. At low tide, like it was right now, the water in the bay totally disappeared and all you could see was the slimy red mud at the bottom. When it was high tide, deep water covered the mud again.

Jay decided to keep on walking. He crossed the tracks and the dusty parking lot to where a metal gate warned people that, if they proceeded, they did so at their own risk. What the heck kind of risk could there be strolling along a dyke trail with hayfields on one side and mud banks on the other?

Far ahead of him were a couple of people walking on the same trail. He couldn't tell if they were coming back to town or still walking further out. It looked like they had a dog with them.

The slight breeze off the mud banks felt good. He grabbed the end of his T-shirt and wiped sweat from his forehead. Grasshoppers, bright green in the summer sun, popped out of the weeds by his feet and leaped to safety. A hawk flew just overhead, barely moving its wings, cruising the dykes and the hayfields for food. Jay could easily distinguish the white feathers under its wings and the brown ones that striped its belly.

In the hour since he had decided to avoid the gym, Jay had managed to block basketball out of his mind almost entirely. Whenever he started to picture Chad or Martin or the basketball game, he forced the image to disappear.

Now he could see that those people out on the dyke were on their way back—it was two guys with a German shepherd. As they came closer, he saw that they were about his age. The dog was smaller than Rudy, and it had a menacing way of prowling with its head low to the ground.

Usually Jay wasn't cautious about dogs, especially ones that reminded him of Rudy. But now he was far away from town, out on the isolated dyke, under the blistering hot sun, surrounded by slippery mud banks and a hayfield. He had only two choices: keep walking forward or turn back. If he turned back all of a sudden it would seem pretty weird, especially if they were just two guys walking with their dog because it was the middle of a hot afternoon and they had nothing else to do.

So Jay kept walking forward.

"Mac! Down!" commanded the dog's owner.

The German shepherd abruptly crouched down, its black eyes studying Jay, its long ears alert.

Jay stood still. "Ah … is your dog friendly?" That sounded so lame.

"Not very," said the owner. He wasn't smiling.

The boy beside him looked about as friendly as the dog. "How come you're out here? Aren't you supposed to be playing basketball or something?"

How did—? Right. Jay was wearing his T-shirt with the Basketball Nova Scotia logo on it. This guy's a detective. "Didn't feel like playing this afternoon."

"Basketball's boring. Am I right? We think basketball's real boring." The two guys nodded at each other, then waited for Jay's response.

"Whatever," said Jay. Who cared what these guys thought? They were acting like lame gangsters in a bad movie.

This situation was getting too weird.

"Hey Mac!" Jay scooped up a smooth stick from the ground and threw it behind him as far as he could. "Fetch!"

The dog bolted out of its crouching position and leapt toward Jay. It blazed past, in pursuit of the stick.

"Hey! What the …"

"We've got a German shepherd. Rudy. He loves chasing sticks. Even more than eating."

Mac pranced back with the stick between his teeth, smiling just the way Rudy smiled when he fetched a ball or a stick.

"Good dog," said Jay. "Good boy."

Mac dropped the stick at his feet, waiting for the next throw.

"You're nuts to try that. My dog could've killed you if he wanted."

"Takes lots of training to make a dog want to kill people." Jay threw the stick again and Mac took off in a flash.

The three boys watched the dog get the stick and trot back again. This time he dropped it in front of his owner. "Leave it, Mac. Let's go."

"Hey," said Jay. "How far does this trail go?"

"Forever."

"How hot is it further out there?"

"It's July. It's sunny. What do you think?"

"Okay if I walk back with you guys?"

The reply from Mac's owner was a shrug of his shoulders as if to say *Who cares?*

Mac was the only friendly one on the walk back toward town. He touched his dry nose to Jay's hand a couple of times, maybe still thinking about the stick.

"Uh-oh," said Mac's owner as they started to cross the dirt parking lot beside the warehouse.

"What?" said the other guy.

"Cops."

A town police car had just turned the corner from the main street and was heading their way.

"Mac, come." He snapped the leash into place on the dog's collar. The two boys and Mac quickly ducked behind the white transfer truck and disappeared around the back of the warehouse.

The police car pulled up beside Jay. Maybe they were after those two guys? What if they thought he was a friend of theirs?

Jay walked over to the car and leaned toward the opened window. "Is there something wrong?"

The officer in the passenger seat reached to open the back door. "We'd like you to get into the car," she said firmly.

"But I don't even know those guys. I was just walking and—"

"You're Jay Hirtle, right."

Hearing his name spoken like that by a police officer made Jay's heart skip a beat. His mouth became even drier than it already was. When he tried to answer, his voice squeaked. He cleared his throat and tried again. "Yes."

"Get in the back, please."

Jay obeyed.

"Looks like you pulled a disappearing act. An hour ago we got a report of a person missing from the basketball camp over at the university."

"I didn't disappear, ma'am. I just went for a walk."

"It's called disappearing when no one knows where you went. You should have told someone."

The officer behind the wheel contacted the dispatch office and reported that they had found Jay and were taking him back to the Acadia gymnasium.

"You can't expect to just go for a walk like that when you're supposed to be at a basketball camp."

The cruiser pulled away from the curb and turned toward the main street.

"I'm sorry. I didn't mean—"

"As long as you're okay, that's the main thing. It's lucky we found you so fast. This could've been a big worry for your parents."

Jay panicked again. "Did they call my parents?"

"No, not yet."

"Do they have to?"

"Maybe not. It depends on why you went off campus by yourself when you're supposed to be playing basketball. That'll be up to your coaches."

Jay looked across the football field and the track as the police car drew closer to the gymnasium. A couple of people were running on the track, despite the heat of the afternoon.

When the cruiser parked at the entrance to the gym, Jay released his seatbelt and started to open the door. "Thanks for driving me back. I'll just go and explain and—"

"Not so fast," said the driver. "We'll be going in with you. This isn't just a taxi service, son."

Oh, great. Nothing like being escorted by two police officers into a crowded gymnasium right in the middle of a basketball game to make a guy wish he could evaporate into thin air.

With an officer on either side of him, Jay walked up the cement steps and into the gym.

7

Lies and Odds

Jamie was standing just inside the gymnasium, waiting for Jay's return. "Thank you, officers. What a relief to have this guy back here safe and sound."

"I'm sorry," said Jay. He found it difficult to look Jamie in the eye. "I didn't think it'd matter if I just went for a walk."

"Well, you thought wrong. It matters a lot. While you're here at basketball camp, we're responsible for you. That means we have to know where you are at all times. Unless you're with a coach, you shouldn't be leaving this campus. Is that clear?"

"Yes, sir." Jay was aware of the fact that most guys in the bleachers weren't concentrating on the action of the basketball game. They were watching what was going on with him and his police escort.

"Any forms we have to fill out on this incident?" asked Jamie.

"That won't be necessary. We're confident it won't happen again." The officer directed that comment at Jay.

"It won't happen, ma'am. I promise."

When the door closed behind the two police officers, Jay turned to Jamie. "Will you be phoning my mom and dad?"

"They should be informed. And I'm going to leave that job

up to you. Tomorrow morning, you let me know how the phone call went. As far as I'm concerned, it was a misunderstanding of basketball camp rules."

"Thank you, sir."

"What's with calling me sir? This is basketball camp, not boot camp. Now join your team in the bleachers and watch the rest of the game."

Jay felt a bit relieved. As he stepped up into the bleachers and made his way to where the Tornadoes were sitting, he tried to look like it was no big deal being picked up by two police officers and delivered back to the gymnasium. He fooled no one.

The Panthers, leading by six points, were in the last quarter of play against the Sharks. With his sweat-soaked T-shirt and his burning red cheeks, Mike looked like he'd played the whole game. Yet he still had his usual high energy, his same keen focus.

Right now, Mike was near the top of the key, evading his guard, freeing himself to receive a short pass. He caught the ball with confidence, but his guard moved in close to trap him. Holding the ball high out of reach, he pivoted, leaving his guard staring at his back. He made a fast return pass to his teammate, who was stalled in the outside lane.

"Move in!" yelled Chad to his brother.

Mike faked left, then ran to the right, positioning himself under the basket. "Over here!" he yelled.

The Sharks swarmed their prey.

Meanwhile, the Panther in the outside lane now had a clear path to the top of the key. Bouncing the ball in four long strides, he was at the line and open for a clean shot. Swish!

A Shark jumped for the ball, but it fell through the net.

What a smooth move! Mike's deception had taken the Sharks completely away from the ball. So preoccupied with the Panthers' highest scorer, they seemed to forget that another player could hit the mark, too. Mike's set-up had worked perfectly.

Jay glanced around at a few of the coaches. Each one took note of Mike's basketball skills, probably deciding right then and there to choose him for the weekend tournament. They'd be crazy not to.

As soon as the game ended, Chad jumped to his feet and joined in the horde of players around his kid brother. The Panther victory had definitely been secured by sixteen-year-old Mike Murphy, a small-town guy on his way to big-time basketball. Jay imagined Mike's picture on a sports page next to a long article about how Murphy was the Centreville rookie to watch.

"Guess you're in trouble with the cops now." Martin tossed the comment at Jay as they stepped down from the bleachers.

"I'm not in trouble with any cops."

"Right." Martin kept on walking.

Jay caught up with him. "You're jumping to conclusions."

"First you say you're gonna improve your game, but you don't mean it. Then you disappear and miss almost the whole game your own roommate's in. When you finally show up, you got a two-cop escort. Looks like trouble to me."

"Well, it's not what it looks like." Jay tried to avoid Martin's eyes. They were like laser beams, going right through him. "I just went for a walk. No big deal. Why should anyone be bugged? I just felt like being alone."

"Usually people got reasons for feelin' like being alone."

Jay was cornered. "If there's reasons, then what's yours? You're always by yourself. Like the other morning when I was running."

"I had my reasons, and they're no one's business."

Now Jay felt like a little kid trying to squirm out of trouble. "Well I have my reasons, and it's no one's business either." Even his voice sounded childish. He was arguing with a guy he admired, a guy willing to be his coach. How weird was that?

Martin's next comment cornered Jay again. "Looks to me like it's the cops' business."

"Jamie told them it was just a misunderstanding."

"That the truth?'

"Sort of."

"Sort of makes it a lie. And lies dig you in so deep you don't know where you are."

"Sounds like you're talking from experience." There he was again, sounding like a whiny kid.

"Yeah, I'm talkin' from experience. But I wasn't the one doing the lying."

Jay couldn't think of anything to answer back. He sensed that Martin was referring to his own father. It added up. His father was the one in the van that first day when Martin walked away without looking back. Then, the next morning, there was Martin all by himself up in the bleachers, probably trying to think things through, things about his father that ticked him off. Lies.

Jamie interrupted the awkward silence that had fallen between Jay and Martin. "So you'll remember that phone call, right?"

"Yes, sir. Soon as supper's over."

"Good. That will settle everything." Jamie smiled and turned to Martin. "Great basketball this afternoon, eh Martin? Some of those guys are definitely varsity material."

"I'd be pickin' Murphy."

"His game was hot today, for sure. So, see you guys tomorrow morning. Last day before the tournament."

"Gotta call home, eh?" said Martin, when Jamie was out of earshot. "Gonna tell the sort-of truth or the real truth?" He left without waiting for Jay to answer.

On his way back to the dorm, Jay organized what he would

tell his parents. *He went for a walk. He wasn't in the mood to watch the basketball game. Besides, how'd he know Mike's team would be picked to play? And for sure he didn't think they'd send the police out looking for him. It was all a misunderstanding.*

Ever since he and Mike had signed up, Jay had been enthusiastic about going to summer basketball camp—a whole week of games and practice and meeting other players and living in a dorm. His parents had even surprised him with the new white-and-blue sneakers for camp. Whether it was his mom or his dad who answered the phone, he didn't want to explain that he was depressed and discouraged.

Martin was wrong. If Jay sort of told the truth, it wouldn't dig him into a deep hole. He'd just tell his parents that he went for a walk and was on his way back to the gym when the police car stopped beside him. It could've been the truth. Maybe he would have headed back there anyway.

"Hey," said Mike. "We're gonna shoot some hoops. Me and Chad and a few other guys. Comin'?"

"Sure. Okay. First I gotta do something. I'll meet you at the gym later."

"Right." Mike pulled a sweatshirt over his head, then bent to tie his sneakers.

"Uh, Mike?"

"Yeah?"

"Sorry I missed most of your game today. I … You were amazing. I mean it. Even Jamie practically said you'd be in the tournament this weekend. I should've been there for the whole thing."

"Maybe I'm the one who got you into trouble. I told Jamie you were nowhere around. I noticed you way over on the other side of the cafeteria eating lunch by yourself. Then you didn't show up at the gym. I figured something was wrong."

"Don't worry about it. I'm not in any trouble. Lighten up. Don't be so serious." Jay grinned.

It took half a second for Mike to get the dig. "Yeah, right." He grinned back.

"Besides, Jamie said it was a misunderstanding. I just went for a walk. Anyway, I was heading for the gym when the police car stopped me."

"Cool. Okay, so see you in the gym."

"Right."

* * *

The phone call home was easy. Jay spoke with his father who said he understood completely.

"Sure it's a safe town," his dad said, "but things can happen anywhere. Even in small towns. That's why your coaches have to be very conscientious about the whereabouts of every single person under their care."

Jay promised to follow the rules, especially the one about not going anywhere without a coach present.

Sam, Gramp, and Jay's mom were over in Richmond checking on the progress of the house renovations.

"We'll be moving back home next Saturday. All we're waiting for now are carpets for your bedroom and Sam's. And another fridge. They sent the wrong size."

When Jay hung up the phone, he felt pretty good. What was the sense of being depressed and discouraged with only one day of camp left? After that, it was the weekend tournament. He could sit back in the bleachers and watch some great basketball. Then, there'd just be one more week before his family moved home to Richmond where life would get back to normal.

There were about a dozen guys in the gym, some shooting hoops and some getting organized for the half-court pickup game. Besides Mike and Chad, Jay didn't actually know most of the guys there. Then he recognized Steve, another Tornado.

"Hey, Steve! How's it goin'?"

"Not bad. You playin'?"

"Yeah."

"Cool."

Chad was going over the rules. "We're four-on-four. No team favourites. There's coaches here and there's basketball players with more experience than other guys. But everyone gets equal playing time."

The more Jay listened, the more amazed he was. Could this be the same guy who usually left him warming the Tornadoes' bench and kept the best players on the floor?

"A game is fifteen points or if it's fifteen to fourteen, the winner is the team that gets a two-point lead. One basket is one point. Everyone got all that? And here's the big thing: each player has to call his own fouls. No faking. No excuses. No bad manners."

Now Jay was sure his ears were deceiving him. Chad—the same guy who screamed from the Tornadoes' bench, who threatened players when they messed up, and who only played to win—here he was talking about *no bad manners*!

"What's with Chad? He's never like this when he's coaching us."

"Nothing to lose in a pickup game, maybe," said Steve. "Some guys are like that—nothing fazes them when they're just foolin' around. But watch out if it's a serious competition."

Serious. There it was again. A reminder to relax. Have some fun, just like Chad was obviously doing.

"Let's number off, starting at this end. Jay, you're one." The other guys continued numbering. "Eleven. Okay. Evens against odds. Evens are blue and odds are orange. Everyone grab a pinnie."

Jay grabbed the familiar orange pinnie. Both Mike and Chad were in blue.

A coin toss gave Blue possession of the ball and the pickup game started. Blue made a quick inbound pass to Mike. Mike angled the ball in a fast bounce pass to Chad. In seconds the first point was scored.

The brothers gave each other a high-five. "Murphy point!" shouted Chad. "And there's more where that came from!"

Orange took the ball under the basket. Blue knocked the pass back out of bounds. Orange made a second try and the ball was in play.

Jay ran down the inside lane, keeping his eyes on the ball. At the top of the key, he caught a long pass. Mike and Chad double-teamed him before he had a chance to even glance toward the basket. He looked through the wall of their bodies, trying to find orange. Chad's large hands captured the basketball and Jay lost possession.

The direction of the action reversed. An Orange point guard blocked Chad's path. He slammed into the guard, knocking him off balance.

"My foul!" yelled Chad, giving the guard a hand up.

Jay watched with disbelief as Chad handed the basketball to his opponent and got ready for the next play. He wasn't smiling, but he wasn't growling either. Too weird. This was definitely a lot more fun.

The pass came to Jay, who was lined up at the low post with two other Oranges. They all had a perfect view of the basket. One guy posted up, raised his hand, and received Jay's pass. He pivoted away from his Blue guard, squared up, and made the jump shot. Game tied.

Three guys substituted in, taking Mike off the floor. Jay and Chad were still in the game. So far, the action wasn't leaving Jay red-faced and out of breath. Half-court in this monstrous gym was the answer. Now, it was a lot more like playing basketball in the smaller gym back home at Richmond Academy.

Blue had the ball. Jay moved in fast and surprised the forward with a quick steal mid-bounce. He kept control of the ball, slowing the action down until he saw a clear path to Orange. His pass was solid. Blue swarmed Orange under the basket.

Jay snuck in behind his teammate and shouted for the ball. He caught the short pass, and without hesitation jumped for a clean layup before the guards could shift position. Orange 2. Blue 1.

The other Orange players crowded Jay, slapping him on the back. "Way to go!"

"Hey! Great move!" Chad gave him a friendly jab in the arm. Then he jogged to the bench so another player could sub in. Mike grabbed the chance and came back into the game.

Jay followed Chad's lead and ran over to the Orange bench. As the pickup game continued, he couldn't help thinking that maybe he'd been jumping to conclusions about Chad. So what if the guy was maybe overly competitive when it came to coaching the Tornadoes? So what if he maybe drank too much the other night? How bad could the guy be if he plays fair in pickup basketball? That had to count for something.

Tomorrow he was going swimming with Chad and Mike. Why be all uptight about that? What're the odds anything bad could happen? It'd be fun.

8

Spud Webb

"Hey, aren't you two supposed to be major opponents today?" said Chad. "Tornadoes verses Panthers. Playoff game." He slid his breakfast tray along the table next to Jay and Mike. "I probably shouldn't even be talking to my own brother before this game."

"I'm on a spy mission to pick up a few Tornado secret plays. You guys talk strategies. Just ignore me."

"Joke all you want, little brother. Panther points'll be in the basement at the end of the game today."

"Better change the subject before we start throwing scrambled eggs," said Mike, laughing. "Great pickup game last night. Real fun."

"Both you guys have basketball talent."

"Well, Mike has anyway," said Jay.

"Don't put yourself down," said Chad. "Age makes a difference, because age translates into experience. Mike's got a year up on you. Oh geez, forgot peanut butter. Be right back."

"Too bad it's raining," said Jay. "I was thinking about how we were supposed to go swimming."

"Maybe it won't rain all day," said Mike. "Hey Chad, think we'll still go swimming later?"

Chad spread peanut butter thickly on his toast. "Sure. Why not?"

"Not much fun if it's raining," said Jay.

"It'll stop. We'll check the situation after the game ... the game the Panthers are gonna lose big time." He grinned at his kid brother.

* * *

Everyone was hyped about two things on the last day of summer basketball camp: the playoff game between the Panthers and the Tornadoes, and the announcement of which six players would be in the weekend tournament. Just about everyone was wearing their Basketball Nova Scotia T-shirt, even though some shirts hadn't made it to a washing machine yet. Jay had tossed his into the wash after the pickup game the previous night, along with everything else in the pile of dirty laundry that had accumulated on the floor of his closet.

The Tornadoes were wearing orange pinnies again. Lucky orange, according to Chad.

The Panthers were in blue.

Chad gave a few last-minute reminders to his team as they gathered in a huddle: "Don't set screens too soon. I wanna see double-teaming, but use caution. Show your hands to who-ever's got the ball. Be ready to receive any pass. Make every shot count." His voice wasn't threatening today, Jay noticed. It sounded firm and confident, like he knew his players were going to deliver their best game.

"This is our last game as the Tornadoes," Chad continued. "I want you guys to know you've been a great team. You prac-tised hard. You played hard. You listened hard. That's why we're in this playoff game. That's why we're going to win this playoff game. Let's hear it!"

Everyone stacked right hands in the centre of the huddle. "GO TORNADOES!!"

Then the playoff game of the Basketball Nova Scotia Summer Camp started.

Mike and Martin shook hands at centre. Jay, playing forward, stood ready to take the tip. Across from him was a Panther forward set for a successful tip from Mike.

Quick whistle, and the ball was up. Martin's fingers found the basketball first and tipped it sharply to Jay. He jumped to receive it, then dribbled fast to the elbow.

Another Tornado blazed up and caught Jay's pass. Martin moved to the three-point line, then came over the screen set up by a guard and showed his hands to receive the ball. The pass was good. Before the Panther guards could block him, Martin slam dunked two points.

"Yes!" screamed Chad from the bench, leaping up and pushing both fists high into the air.

The Panthers took the ball out of bounds under the basket. Martin stuck to Mike like glue, watching the ball and keeping in sync with Mike's movements the whole time. The pass went to a Panther on the other side, and the action turned toward the Tornado basket.

"Stop these guys!" yelled Chad.

Jay raced beside the Panther forward, trying his best to keep him out of the play. By now, his breath was quick and his lungs were stinging. Two days without running practice felt like two years. Sweat crawled through his hair and down his neck.

Mike made a pivot break from Martin and, in that split second, received the pass. Steve moved into position for a double-team play with Martin. They had Mike blocked. A reverse pass was impossible. The referee's whistle blew.

Tornado ball.

Steve took the basketball out, pausing only long enough to see that his team had their positions. The inbound pass came fast to Ronny at center. He dribbled to the left of the key, keeping Martin inside his field of vision.

Two Panther guards moved in to double-team Martin. Ronny lost sight of him, but saw Jay just inside the key near the throw line. He sent the ball in a snap pass to Jay.

Immediately, Jay was surrounded by blue. He faked a jump, then pivoted left. Without hesitation, he went up for his shot. Too much force. The ball hit the rim and slammed back over the heads of all the players under the basket.

Martin saw the ricochet before it even happened. He ran back, unguarded, and was ready to catch the ball near top of the key. He jumped and delivered a perfect two-point swish through the hoop.

Tornadoes 4. Panthers zilch.

Chad invented a new dance all by himself in front of the Tornadoes' bench.

Martin was immediately surrounded by orange.

The Panther coach called for a time out.

Back at the Tornadoes' bench, Chad didn't even mention Jay's missed shot. "Excellent stuff! Excellent! Take a short break, Martin. Let's save you some energy. Chris, you're in. Steve, take centre position."

Martin glugged half a bottle of water. He grabbed a towel to wipe his face, then left the towel draped around his neck. He couldn't stop grinning.

Finally, thought Jay, Martin's where he wants to be, doing what he wants to do. Nothing was in his way. No other players could come near him for basketball talent. And Chad obviously realized that Martin brought gold to the Tornadoes—he was definitely treating him with the respect he deserved.

The game ended before the Panthers had a chance to haul their score out of the basement, just as Chad had predicted.

It was still raining as the basketball players and their coaches walked to the dining hall for lunch.

"Never say never," said Chad, still bolstered by the Tornado win. "I say we'll get to go swimming."

* * *

Jamie stood at the center of the gymnasium next to a long table spread with six varsity uniforms: two white-and-maroon for Saint Mary's University; two black-and-gold for Dalhousie, and two red-and-blue for Acadia. Players in the bleachers imagined themselves wearing one of those uniforms on Saturday and Sunday.

Even though he knew he didn't have a hope of being selected, Jay could picture himself in the red-and-blue Acadia basketball uniform. Varsity basketball. Amazing!

This time, Jamie's speech was brief. He thanked everyone for bringing friendship and respect to Basketball Nova Scotia's summer camp. He said that this camp saw some of the finest young basketball talent Nova Scotia has ever had.

Jay felt good to be included in all that talk about friendship, and respect, and talent. He had come close to really messing up big time by wandering off alone; but Jamie had obviously forgotten about that. A misunderstanding. Why not?

Also, Jay had had the privilege of being coached, even if it was just for two days, by the basketball camp's top player. For sure, he'd never forget the running tips Martin had given him, and the friendship. Especially the friendship.

"Here's the moment we've been waiting for. Six players will represent all of us this weekend in the Alumni Invitational

Basketball Tournament. Two will play for Acadia. Two for Dalhousie. And two for Saint Mary's. And here are the names ..."

Jay was sitting beside Mike. "Good luck. But you don't
need it." He glanced over at Martin who was looking straight
ahead, expressionless.

"For Acadia Alumni, our two players are: Buck Simm and
Mike Murphy."

Jay gave Mike a congratulations slam on the arm. In the
noise of the applause, Mike made his way down from the
bleachers and over to the table at the centre of the court. The
two players received their red-and-blue varsity basketball uniforms as if they were royal robes.

The Saint Mary's players were announced next, and the
Tornadoes cheered for Steve as he accepted his white-and-
maroon colours.

"Finally, on the Dalhousie University Alumni team, we will
be represented by ... Logan McLennan and Martin Carvery!"

Jay jumped up again, cheering and clapping. "Way to go,
Martin!" He touched two fingers against his lips and blasted a
shrill whistle into the air.

Summer basketball camp shifted into overdrive. After five
days of drills and plays, victories and defeats, everyone now
geared up for two full days of exceptional basketball with university players. Jay couldn't wait to see his friends wearing varsity colours. When Dal played Acadia, Jay would have to make
the big decision about which team to cheer loudest for.

"Hey, Martin. Way to go! I knew you'd get picked."

"You mighta made it too, Jay."

"Not in a million years."

"Like I said, you don't know Spud Webb."

"Oh yeah. That guy. Who is he anyway?"

"He's you."

"Come on, Martin, forget the riddles."

"Spud Webb's an NBA player with an amazing vertical jump. Forty-two inches. I mean it. He beat out guys who were giants in a slam dunk championship."

"So why'm I supposed to know him?"

"The guy's five-seven. Like you." Martin let that interesting fact sink in. "Maybe he really isn't like you, though. Spud Webb stuck with his dream to play basketball. Even when people told him he'd never make it."

That stung. But Jay let it go. Now that basketball camp was coming to an end, he didn't want to create a wider gap between him and Martin. They had been friends for a couple of days. Maybe they could still be friends.

"I'll be playing basketball. It's just—well I'm not varsity material."

"Yet."

Jay smiled. As a coach, Martin didn't quit.

* * *

Jay and Mike had given up on the idea of going swimming. The drizzling rain had lasted until dinnertime; and later they got distracted by NBA basketball videos. Powerful giant arms! Amazing long legs! Shots that couldn't miss! Basketball moves that always worked!

"So here's where you guys are." Chad came into the TV room, dangling his car keys from his finger. "We goin' swimmin' or what?"

"Isn't it too late?" said Mike. "It's almost dark."

"Maybe tomorrow," said Jay.

"Forget tomorrow. I got other things to do tomorrow. It's now or never."

Jay was about to say *never* when Mike looked over at him, "What d'you think?"

"Uh … sure. Why not?"

"Anyone else wanna come?" asked Chad. "We got room for two more."

"You guys're nuts," said one guy.

Everyone else in the TV room looked too comfortable to move.

"I'll be in the car. You guys get your stuff. Let's get rollin'."

9

"Look out!"

Jay dug through the drawer for his swimsuit, grabbed his jacket out of the closet and pulled a towel off the hook behind the door. It felt too weird heading out at night to go swimming. But he didn't say anything. Why look like a wimp when you didn't have to?

"Hurry up. Chad's down in the car already," said Mike.

Jay was right behind him.

"Hey, you guys, look. Full moon, like I said. This is gonna be a blast." Chad started the car as Mike and Jay jumped in.

"How long does it take to get there?" asked Jay.

"Forty minutes, maybe. We go over two exits and then down this back road that takes us to the mill. It's not far. It'll be worth it."

Jay settled into the back seat. He thought about the drive to basketball camp from Centreville with Chad passing everything in sight and fishtailing all over the place. Tonight, there was hardly any traffic. Good. Nothing for Chad to pass.

They took the exit ramp and then turned left, driving up the gradual incline of South Mountain and then starting down the other side. About halfway down, Chad slowed the car and made a right turn onto a dirt road.

"Lucky we had rain today," said Chad. "The dust's a real pain when this road's dry."

Then he leaned forward and looked up through the front windshield, his face just about on the steering wheel. "Guys, check this out." Chad slowed the car, then twisted the small lever beside the steering wheel. The headlights blinked out.

"Wha—"

"Wait for it."

In seconds, Jay's eyes adjusted and the road ahead washed with milky light. He gradually distinguished more details: plumes of grass reaching up out of the ditch; pine branches with long needles; spruce trees and maples; small rocks piled at the side of the gravel road; a few puddles from the morning's rain.

Chad pointed overhead.

Jay wound down the window and looked up into the white face of a brilliant full moon. It melted the black sky into royal blue. It spilled light down into the forest and along the isolated road. Around the moon was an enormous white circle, a cloudy ring. What did Gramp always say when there was a ring around the moon? Something about a storm warning.

Chad drove slowly on, guided only by the full moon.

This is kind of cool, thought Jay. *A totally unreal place. Like being in a movie.* Still, he was on edge, as though a car, coming out of nowhere, might suddenly appear in front of them. Or something else. A person walking alone on this secluded road under the ghostly light of the moon.

The road ahead faded suddenly to blackness. Chad quickly flicked the headlights back on. "Must be clouds." He stepped on the gas. "Anyway, what d'ya think of that?"

"Too cool," said Mike.

"Weird," said Jay.

The car kicked up gravel behind its wheels. Abruptly, the

thick forest ended and now fields of hay were on either side of them. Near the top of a hill was a farmhouse, barely distinguishable at the end of the long driveway. One bright yellow porch light beamed into the night.

As they drove on, the moon came out from behind the clouds, illuminating the fields of hay and the farmhouse on the hill. Jay let his head drop against the back of the seat and gazed out the window. Everything looked so quiet and peaceful.

They finally turned right and bumped along a narrow road that ended at the mill and the pond. Chad left the headlights on so they could get out of the car and have a look around.

"Cool, eh?"

"Kinda spooky," said Mike.

"Go on. Spooky? This place isn't spooky. It's just deserted."

"How old's this mill?" asked Jay.

"Who knows? Fifty years. A hundred, maybe."

"That road's for sure a hundred years old," said Jay. His stomach still felt a bit squeamish from bouncing and lurching from side to side.

"People come here to swim or have campfires and stuff. They at least keep trees and junk off the road."

In the beam of the headlights, Jay saw a fire pit surrounded by old stumps and fallen tree trunks that were used as seats. Lots of broken glass was in the pit. Chip bags and other garbage were scattered here and there.

"Time to get wet," said Chad, going back to the car and switching off the headlights. The moon filled the night with milky light. "Don't even feel the water. Take my word for it— it's cold. Just follow me up on that wall and go for it."

They peeled on their bathing suits and threw their towels onto the rocks near the edge of the pond.

The dilapidated mill was made of stone and cement, with

battered wooden doors and window frames. The old wheel, divided into rows of wooden slats, barely hung in place on immense rusted hinges. Those slats had once scooped up water, turned the wheel, then splashed the water back into the pond. They were useless now.

The top of the cement wall was wide enough for easy walking, as long as you held your arms out for balance. It was about six or seven feet above the pond.

"Don't think. Just jump," said Chad. "Okay, baby brother, last one in's a—"

Splash! Mike's body hit the water, leaving Chad high and dry. Jay howled with laugher.

Chad wasn't going to be left behind for long. Out he leaped toward the centre of the pond, sinking down with a great spray of water.

Jay looked into the darkness and tried not to think. He jumped from the cement wall into the black water below. Splash! Down and down and down through the cold he went, his legs curled under him and his eyes squeezed shut. Then up he swam out of the blackness to the surface. "Waahoo!"

"Ain't that somethin'?" yelled Chad.

Mike was already swimming back toward the cement wall.

"It's freezing!" shouted Jay.

"You'll get used to it!"

Jay swam to the edge of the pond and waded toward the cement wall. His lips were shivering, probably turning a shade of midnight blue by now. Goosebumps coated his whole body. Who cared? This was fun!

Balancing on the wall, he looked down past his toes curled at the edge. When he moved his foot, small bits of cement broke away and sprinkled down into the pond. The moon and the clouds in the sky matched the moon and the clouds reflected in the water. On the surface of the pond, he saw the dark arm of a cloud reach across the edge of that perfect circle of white light. The arm slid past, and once more the moon floated undisturbed.

Jay leaped. Down he splashed through the clouds and the moon, sinking like a stone into the blackness. Up he floated to the surface again. Although his body shivered in the cool air and the even colder water, he was having a ball.

The night filled with thunderous splashes, with dares, with laughter, with more shouts and challenges. It was as if the mill, the cement wall, and the pond were all inside a gigantic dome with walls painted in the thick, black shapes of trees and an eerie replica of a full moon. Their shouts and laughter echoed inside the dome.

"Let's all try to jump at the exact same time!" yelled Mike.

They lined up on the wall, knees bent, ready for the countdown.

"One." Mike was in the middle. He looked right and then left.

"Two."

Jay put his elbows back and lifted up on his toes. He stared straight ahead into the blue-black night.

"Three!"

They were in the air together, then they hit the pond with a tremendous triple splash. The water around Jay churned with thousands of bubbles. He pushed up through the foam to the surface, gulping for air and shaking water out of his eyes and hair. He was alone. The pond settled to a rippled mirror, catching the moonlight and sliding it in larger and larger circles toward the dark banks.

Suddenly the ripples split open. One head, then the other, popped up and arms smashed through the spray.

"Eeeeooooow!" screamed Chad.

Mike floated on his back and kicked water into a foaming trail.

When they all waded back to the mill, Jay picked up his towel and wrapped it tightly around his shoulders. "Maybe we should head back."

"What're you in such a hurry for?"

"I'm freezing."

"Wimp."

"Me too," said Mike, pulling his towel around himself. "I say we get going."

"You're both wimps."

They stripped out of their bathing suits and hauled on jeans and sweatshirts. Jay thought about putting on his jacket, too, but changed his mind. Once the car was going and the heater was on, they'd get warmer.

Chad backed up the car and turned toward the mill road. The headlights bounced past the dilapidated mill, the cement wall, and the quiet pond. The beam blazed across the thick wall of spruce trees until it settled on the rutted road.

Mike rolled his window all the way down, letting in the cool night air. He stuck his elbow out as if they were cruising along on a hot summer's day.

The car lurched and bumped from side to side, splashing through shallow puddles, scraping in the deep ruts. There was a tunnel of light in front of them, illuminating the road and the tangle of spruce trees and bushes on either side. Pitch black night loomed all around the tunnel.

Jay shoved his towel and wet bathing suit to the far side of the back seat and lay his jacket beside him. He readjusted his safety belt. There was nothing much to see out his window. Occasionally, a ragged branch reached out and clawed at the side of the car.

When the potholed road straightened out into a wider, smoother section, Chad stepped on the gas.

"Now you see it." Chad laughed and snapped off the headlights. "Now you don't."

Mike laughed at Chad's pseudo joke.

It took a few seconds before Jay could see anything. When his eyes adjusted to the moonlight, the dirt road was a barely visible path through the darkness. He sat up and focused straight ahead, as if he could be an extra pair of eyes guiding that car through the night. Why did Chad have to pull this stupid stunt again? His body shivered, and Jay knew it wasn't because of swimming in that freezing water.

"Look out!"

Mike's scream was a split second ahead of Chad's reaction. He slammed on the brakes and hauled the steering wheel hard to the left. The car spun sideways. The front tire hit the brink of the embankment and Chad lost control. The car careened downward, smashing against enormous boulders at the bottom of the embankment.

Then there was only darkness and silence.

In the unnatural quiet, Jay could still hear the violent sounds of scraping and splintering, and that final crash when the car hit the boulders. His right shoulder hurt. But he was still strapped into his seatbelt. Nothing felt broken. Nothing felt cut. The wet towel and bathing suit were on the floor by his feet. His jacket was in his lap.

A vague image started to form in his mind. Something he thought he saw just before the car swerved. What was it? A flash of movement. Brown and white. A tail and long legs bounding away through the thick bushes.

A deer.

Jay could barely make out Chad in the front seat, rubbing his forehead. He couldn't see Mike at all. He snapped off his seatbelt and leaned forward. Mike was there, still strapped in, but tilted awkwardly against the opened window. He looked dead.

The car had crashed without flipping over, but it tilted sharply against the massive boulders. The nearby sound of splashing told Jay they were close to the edge of a stream. He could smell water, cool and fresh. He also noticed the pungent smell of gas and oil.

"Chad, turn off the car! Chad, you hear me?"

"Yeah. The … I—"

Jay's eyes adjusted a bit more to the darkness. "Is it off?"

Chad found the ignition. "Yeah."

"Good. Now we gotta check Mike."

Chad opened his door and crawled out as Jay climbed from the backseat. The moonlight grew brighter through the trees.

"You all right?"

"Yeah. I'm pretty sure." From the vague hesitation in Chad's voice, Jay knew he was in shock.

"Let me check him." Jay inched across the driver's seat. There was a strong pulse in Mike's neck. What a relief! "Mike! Can you hear me?" He felt Mike's forehead. "He's bleeding. Hand me my jacket."

Chad, stunned by shock, did exactly as he was told.

Jay put his jacket over Mike and tucked it up around his neck, hoping it would give at least some warmth. He still wasn't moving.

Jay tried to think quickly and calmly. All he could hear was the frantic sound of his own heart pounding in his ears.

10

The Run

Jay could see that the car was not in danger of rolling any further. It had come to rest against some large boulders at the edge of the stream. He was hoping those boulders weren't the reason Mike had blood on his face.

The stream bubbled and splashed over rocks and over roots of trees gnarled along the bank. The moon came out again from behind the clouds, changing the black night to a milky blue. Through the branches of the tall trees, Jay could see there weren't many more clouds. This was the kind of lucky break they needed right now.

He grabbed a towel and made his way through bushes to the bank of the stream. He dipped part of the towel into the cold water and hurried back to the car. Chad was kneeling on the driver's seat checking Mike.

"Here, wipe the blood off. Can you see where he's cut?"

Chad gently wiped Mike's forehead. "Can't tell. It's in his hair, I think."

"Much blood?"

"A bit. Might've stopped, though."

"Good." Jay knew there was no time to waste. "I'll get help. You stay with Mike. Keep him warm. Keep talking to him."

"Where'll you go?" Chad's voice was thin.

"Any houses further down that main road?"

"I don't know," said Chad. "There might be."

"Can't chance it. I'm going back the way we came. There's a farm I saw."

"How far back?"

"Far." Jay didn't let himself think about the distance, the night, or the isolation he would feel on the dirt road. "Say his name a lot."

"Okay."

"Starting now."

Jay turned and ran. His legs were unsteady under him, and a cold shiver ran through his body. For a few seconds, he could still hear Chad's voice, just bits of what he was saying to his kid brother. "Can you hear me, Mike? Jay ... help, Mike ... all right ... Mike."

Before he was even fifty metres away, Jay tripped and fell, his two palms scrapping along sharp rocks and his right knee taking the brunt of his weight. He scrambled to his feet again. His whole body shook, more with fright than injury. He brushed the grit from his hands and knees and felt the sticky warmth of blood oozing from a small gash on one knee. He thought of Mike.

Jay knew what had caused that fall. Nervousness. Extreme nervousness. He had to calm himself, take control. He gulped three deep breaths, blowing the air out of his lungs, trying to steady his breathing. Then he started running again.

The car and the two brothers were now far behind him. Jay was alone, looking down at his long shadow cast ahead of him by the full moon. He could hear the rushing babble of the stream in the woods nearby. The old mill road was pocked with ruts filled with rain, small pools ready to trip him.

He wanted his heart rate to slow down and the trembling in

his legs to dissolve. He wanted his sneakers to miss every rut and rock that might throw him off balance. He wanted to be running up that farm lane, seconds away from help.

The sound of the stream grew fainter as the mill road curved deeper into the woods toward the main gravel road. Jay listened to his sneakers against the dirt surface and thought of the track. But this wasn't like running on the track at all. Here, he could barely distinguish between shadows and ruts, except when puddles caught the eerie moonlight and turned silver. Nothing was predictable on this isolated, darkened road.

An unfamiliar creaking noise came from the forest. Jay lurched sideways as if to avoid collision with … what? His heart leaped, but he didn't stop running. There was the creaking again. And again. He recognized the sound this time: one heavy branch scraping against another. Looking up, he saw the highest trees heaving and swaying gently. A slight breeze must be moving across the top of the forest.

In that instant, he stumbled sideways, one foot smashing into the other. Somehow he kept his balance and didn't fall.

He tried to concentrate on his shadow as it moved in front of him and hoped no clouds were crawling toward the moon to smother its light.

There! The mill road ended just up ahead.

He turned left onto the wider road and picked up a bit more speed. But this road had recently been graded, leaving clumps of gravel and dirt in heaps along the sides. He tried to find a place in the middle where he wasn't as likely to twist an ankle and fall.

Jay's shadow ran beside him now. It made him think of Martin, keeping pace with him at the track and coaching him. *Don't watch your sneakers. Hold your head up. Listen to your feet. Pick up the rhythm. Match it to your breath. In-out. In-out. That's it. You got it.*

He did what Martin's voice told him to do, concentrating on his running, blocking out the sounds and erasing the image of Mike with his eyes closed and his head bleeding.

The forest on either side of the road was black with tall spruce trees. Silent. If any creatures were awakened by the pounding of Jay's sneakers on the gravel road, they might lift their heads and wonder. When the running sound was gone, they would tuck their heads back into their fur or feathers and drift back to sleep. An owl on a high branch might blink, then listen again for more woodland noises.

Someone might be driving across the countryside on this gravel road tonight. Jay wished for that with all his strength. He thought about how surprised they'd be to see him running by himself. He'd jump up and down and wave his arms in the glare of their headlights. They'd stop, and he'd explain as fast as he could, pushing the words out in gasps. They'd probably even have a cellphone.

Maybe, by now, Mike had opened his eyes. Chad might be telling him about how Jay was running to get help.

The moonlight wavered and Jay's shadow blurred. Clouds. He didn't dare risk another fall by glancing up to see if it was just a small bunch or a whole bank of clouds. All he could see right now were the dense black lines of forest on either side of him. He looked straight ahead into the darkness and tried to stay on the road between those pitch-black walls. A milky light spilled around him momentarily and then faded again.

Jay ran on through the black night.

All his attention was focused on getting to that farmhouse somewhere up ahead. Without the moon to guide him, his pace was now slower. He couldn't think about that. He had to make sure he didn't fall again and pull a ligament or twist an ankle, injuries that would stop him here on this remote road.

He'd be useless to Mike.

Finally, his shadow came back. It slid along the road and warped over the small mounds of gravel piled near the edge.

Pick a spot up ahead. Not far. Say, the end of those bleachers. Okay? Now, double your speed. Go! Go! Go! Go!

Jay's shadow raced beside him. Faster, faster, faster. His feet hit the road double time, finding an even surface in the moonlight.

Good! Now slow up a bit. Listen to your breath. Get your rhythm. There!

He pictured telling Martin about running in the dark. He'd describe how sometimes he had help from the moon, and how other times it was like running into a black tunnel with your eyes almost shut. Then he'd finally tell how he found the farmhouse and got help for Mike.

The pain in Jay's chest and the trembling in his legs seemed to be less extreme now. His breathing was more even and he was getting used to the gravel road underfoot.

You'll get a second wind. Like your fuel tank's topped up. Martin was right. Jay definitely felt that second wind. He could pump his arms faster now. His legs pushed ahead with longer strides. Even on this empty country road, he wasn't afraid to run and run and run.

Race me, Jay.

Okay, Sam. I'll give you a head start. Ready. Set. Go!

He picked up speed, matching his quick breaths in and out to the sound of his feet moving forward and forward. This time he couldn't let Sam win the race. Jay inhaled deeply as he continued to run. The country smells were cool, musky, green. He could hear the stream again, meandering somewhere in the darkness.

Now, he was running on automatic. Automatic breath in and

out, automatic fists clenched, automatic elbows bent, automatic arms back and forth at his sides, automatic quick pace of one foot in front of the other. He couldn't feel the sting from the scrapes and scratches on his hands and knees anymore. He couldn't feel his legs moving under him.

Just in time, he saw the narrow wooden bridge directly ahead. Moonlight glistened on two wet centreboards. He aimed for one of those boards. In three strides—thump, thump, thump—he was on the other side. Through the wide gaps in the crossbeams, he had seen the black water moving a few metres beneath him. Too close.

Jay thought of a number: 150. He picked up speed, racing his shadow in the moonlight and counting each stride. One, two, three, four, five, six … double-time speed, until 47, 48, 49, 150!

Slower now. Back on automatic.

Sweat trickled down his temples.

Blood on Mike's face.

Jay's shadow melted again into the dark night. Clouds had drifted across the moon.

Numbers were still in his head, counting without purpose in the dark. For a split second, he didn't register the break in the forest and the amber glow on the side of a hill.

A porch light! The farmhouse!

He raced up the lane with a last burst of energy. No lights were on inside. The small doghouse under a tangled apple tree was deserted too, the dog's leash lying in the grass.

Jay pounded on the front door. Was everyone asleep? Seconds were wasting. He pounded again. Was no one home?

He picked up a round-painted rock from the border of a flower garden and smashed the glass in the door. He reached inside and opened the lock on the handle.

Nothing moved inside the house.

In the kitchen, he found a phone, dialed 911, and blurted out his story in quick gasps. His lungs burned. Tremors shook his body.

"Stay on the line," said the dispatcher.

He could hear her connect with the Mounties.

"We have a patrol car not far from that mill road. They'll be with your friends in ten minutes. Stay by the phone. I'll get back to you as soon as the officers call in."

Jay collapsed into a chair at the kitchen table and put his head down on his hands.

Everything was so unreal. Had he actually just been in an accident? Had Mike really been hurt? Had he raced along a deserted country road in the middle of the night? Here he was now, in someone else's kitchen, someone who would come home and find their front door smashed by some stranger.

He went to the sink and poured himself a drink of water. Then another one.

He sat down again and stared at the pictures on the fridge door: kids at Christmas, kids blowing out birthday candles, kids at the beach, school pictures of kids leaning their arms on fake wooden fences. One picture showed a black dog on a leash beside the doghouse.

Rudy.

Sam.

Mom and Dad and Gramp and Sam and Rudy.

It felt peaceful just to think of their names like that. What was his family doing right now? They didn't know he had been racing with his own shadow through the country darkness as fast as he possibly could, trying to get help for Mike.

Was he too late?

Maybe Mike actually did open his eyes the way Jay had pictured. Or maybe he was still unconscious, getting colder and colder in the damp darkness.

Jay didn't even know how long it had taken him to run from the car to this farmhouse. Must have been at least forty minutes. It felt like forever.

The accident was Chad's fault. Jay knew it. Chad knew it. If Mike regained consciousness, he would know it, too. Would he try to make excuses for his older brother again? Would he ask Jay to help with another cover-up?

There was no way Jay would do that. Absolutely no way.

And what if Mike didn't regain consciousness? How would Chad feel when he was blamed for his own brother's death?

Jay shook that thought out of his head. The car didn't flip all the way over. And Chad had said the bleeding looked like it had stopped. But those boulders—.

The phone rang and Jay grabbed it.

11

Personal Best

Jay sat nervously on a plastic chair in the emergency waiting room. His head ached and his legs still felt wobbly from running. Chad stood next to a window, looking out into the night, waiting for his parents to get there. Three others were in the room: a man holding an infant wrapped in a quilt that had ducks on it; a woman beside him, brushing her hand across the baby's forehead and tucking the quilt under its chin; and a man sitting alone with a bloodstained towel around his hand. The Mounties who had driven Jay to the hospital had now left.

When Chad's parents arrived, he would have a lot of explaining to do. Maybe they wouldn't ask many questions, they'd be so relieved to see that at least one of their sons wasn't injured in the car accident.

The nurse who had greeted Jay when he'd first arrived now walked back into the waiting room.

"Is Mike okay?" Jay asked the question before Chad had a chance to speak.

"The doctors are still with him. Everything looks positive, so far." He turned to the couple with the baby. "Mr. and Mrs. Windsor, a doctor will see little Clara now. Come with me."

"Rough night," said the man with the bloodstained towel.

"Things always seem worse at night, though. Is your friend the one they just brought in the ambulance?"

"Yeah," said Jay. "He's his brother." He nodded in Chad's direction, but Chad didn't turn around.

"Car accident?"

"Yeah. There was this deer…"

"Had that happen to me once. They come outta nowhere."

"Yeah."

"Your brother'll be fine," he said to the back of Chad's head. "The nurse wouldn't't've said everything looked positive if it wasn't true."

Chad still didn't respond.

"I got brothers. Four of 'em. I know how you feel."

The nurse came into the waiting room again and beckoned to Jay. "Let's get you looked after now."

When Jay returned, he had three blue stitches across his right knee. The cut was throbbing. All the grit had been cleaned off his other knee and the palms of his hands. Orange antiseptic stained the shallow cuts.

The couple and their baby had just left. Jay could see them heading toward the hospital parking lot. The man with the bloodstained towel wasn't in his chair anymore. Probably being seen by a doctor, finally. No other patients had come into the emergency waiting room.

Jay checked the clock on the wall. 1:06. His father would be halfway here by now. The Murphys might arrive sooner. He sat down and tried to get comfortable in the narrow plastic chair.

Chad was still at the window, staring out. His silence suddenly infuriated Jay.

"This is all your fault!"

"I know." Chad didn't turn around. His voice was so quiet Jay didn't hear him.

"You caused the accident. Admit it. It wasn't that deer's fault."

"I know."

"You always gotta be so big. Oh look at me. I can drive with the lights off. I can speed on back roads. Now, there's Mike. And all those doctors. And it's your fault!"

"I know."

Jay finally realized what Chad was saying. He heard the desperation in his whispered words. It had been Chad's kid brother beside him in the car, bleeding and not moving. It was his kid brother lying on an examination table right now with doctors all around him. No one needed to shout blame at Chad. He already blamed himself.

"Mike'll be okay," said Jay. He could see Chad's solemn face reflected in the darkened window. "Don't worry."

Headlights beamed into the hospital parking lot from the street. "There's Mom and Dad," said Chad.

The nurse came back to the waiting room again. "You can see your brother now. Only for a minute, though."

"Mom and Dad just got here. Should I wait for them?"

"You'll be back out here by the time they walk across the parking lot. It's better not to have too many people at once."

Chad glanced over at Jay, as if looking for a reason to avoid seeing Mike. "Okay, then," he said and followed the nurse.

Alone in the waiting room, Jay felt as if he was holding his breath. Too much had happened tonight. Too much seemed unreal.

Chad and the nurse returned just as Mr. and Mrs. Murphy walked in.

"Chad! Oh thank God, thank God you're all right." Mrs. Murphy wrapped her arms around her older son. His father stood beside them with one hand gently touching Chad's back. "Where's Michael?" Her voice reminded Jay of someone lost and confused, on the edge of hysteria.

"I just saw him. He's awake. But he's kinda groggy, like."

"Mrs. Murphy. Mr. Murphy," said the nurse. "I'll take you to your son. Please follow me. Chad, you'll need to stay here for now."

"So how is he?" asked Jay when the door closed behind Chad's parents and the nurse.

"Groggy." Chad sat in a chair across from Jay. "He said he remembered the deer."

"What about the blood we saw on him?"

"They shaved part of his head, by his ear. He's got stitches. The doctor said it was good that I kept talking to him, saying his name like that." Chad still wasn't making eye contact with Jay. "They said he'll have to stay here in the hospital a couple days. For observation." He stared down at the covers of ancient magazines tossed on a table beside his chair. Then he looked straight at Jay. "You saved my brother's life." Tears glazed his eyes, then spilled down his cheeks. "I … I don't know what I'd do if..."

Jay thought of Sam. "You saved Mike's life, too. By being there while I ran for help."

Chad wiped his eyes with his fingertips and brushed his hands along the knees of his jeans. "He didn't move. And he was getting colder and colder and there wasn't anything else dry to cover him with. I told him over and over that you were getting help. I tried not to even think about how far away that farm was."

"Me, too. I just kept concentrating on running and not falling down."

"When I saw those Mounties comin', with their flashing lights, I couldn't believe it."

The Mounties. So far, very few questions had been asked. But Jay knew the entire story would soon have to be explained.

"You gonna tell what happened? What really happened?"

He had made a decision and he wasn't about to change his mind. "Because if you're not, I am."

No way a person could fake the expression on Chad's face. "I could've killed my own brother. The least I can do now is tell what I did."

"Right. 'Cause things would just get worse if you lied. Like digging holes you can't get out of."

Chad's parents came back to the waiting room, still looking stressed but definitely feeling a bit relieved. His mom put her arms around him, holding tightly, her eyes closed.

"Did he talk to you, Mom?"

"Mostly listened. But he said he remembers that you stayed with him all that time." She turned to Jay. "And that you ran to get help."

"On the way here, we passed that farm," said Chad. "Had to be at least eight kilometres from where the car was. I don't know how you did it, man. In the dark like that and everything."

"Most of the time the moon was out and I could see pretty good."

"Our family is still a whole family because of you." Mrs. Murphy hugged Jay. Her face felt wet against his cheek. "We are so lucky. So grateful."

Mr. Murphy shook Jay's hand firmly. "There are no words to say how grateful … Thank you just doesn't seem enough. Your run helped save Mike's life."

* * *

When Jay's father arrived at the hospital, there was a repeat performance of hugging and shaking hands and tears and praise. The Murphys had already phoned Jamie to let him know what had happened. Plans were made for them to stay at a nearby hotel. They wouldn't leave Kentville until Mike was ready to go home with them.

As Jay and his father drove into the parking lot in front of Chipman House, Jamie was coming out of the dorm.

"Dad, this is Jamie, one of our main coaches. This is my Dad."

"Mr. Hirtle—"

"Brian."

"Your son is a hero tonight. Guess no one has to tell you that. I just explained to some of the boys what the Murphys told me over the phone. Jay, what you've done has unequivocally avoided a tragedy for this basketball camp. No question about it." He reached out and firmly shook Jay's hand. "We all thank you very much. Words just don't express it enough. We want you and your family to come back here on Sunday afternoon, if you will. We'll plan for a special thank you as we close the tournament."

"Sounds good to me," said his dad, his arm proudly around Jay's shoulder. "Wouldn't mind catching a basketball game here. Be like old times. What do you think, son?"

"Um, sure." Jay had a funny feeling the *special thank you* Jamie was talking about would involve embarrassing speeches. He hoped he wouldn't have to make one.

"You all right to go get your stuff? I'll stay here and speak with Jamie for a minute."

The first person he saw when he got up to the third floor was Martin, standing at his opened door. "Jay, my man! That was some run! Jamie told us all about it. Had to be your personal best."

Jay just shrugged his shoulders. It was even more depressing to hear Martin praising him. "I was in that car, too. I didn't open my mouth when Chad drove like an idiot." He went into his room to begin packing, and Martin followed him.

"But Mike's gonna be okay. And that's because of you."

"I wouldn't've had to run if I'd said something to Chad. He even turned off the headlights. Driving with just the moon to see by. And I'm in the back seat saying nothing. Now Jamie's got this idea to have some speeches and stuff at the end of the tournament. I'm no hero. I'll feel like an idiot."

"So, okay, you messed up when you didn't say anything to Chad. But that doesn't make you an idiot. You ran for help. Take the glory."

Jay had all his things crammed into his backpack and duffle bag. He looked over at Mike's empty bed and his shorts and T-shirt on the floor beside it. "May as well pack up Mike's stuff for him. Chad'll probably come to get it tomorrow."

Martin went to the closet and started hauling clothes off hangers and off the closet floor.

"Dad says we'll come back on Sunday to catch a game. Probably our whole family'll come." Jay squirmed a bit, mentioning his dad. Maybe Martin's own father wouldn't be there to watch the tournament. Or maybe he'd tell Martin he'd be there and then he wouldn't show up. "Wait'll you meet Sam. He's nuts, but he's fun."

"Will Rudy be there, too? Or maybe I could just phone him up sometime." Martin grinned and gave Jay a punch in the arm.

Jay put his backpack and duffel bag into his dad's van. Jamie had left, and by the look on his father's face they had had enough time to make a few embarrassing plans for Sunday. "Can we go back over to the hospital? I need to see how Mike is before we head for Gramp's."

They drove down the campus hill to the deserted main street. Jay looked across the intersection at the parking lot and the university gymnasium illuminated by huge floodlights.

Although he couldn't see the track, he could distinguish the goalposts, stark white against the black sky. He and Martin had practised there for just two mornings. That seemed like a hundred years ago, when there was a ton of stuff that hadn't happened, when there was a ton of stuff Jay didn't know.

Martin was right about a lot of things, and he was a major good coach, that was for sure. But he was wrong about one thing: the run had definitely not been Jay's personal best. Facing up to Chad and then facing the fact that he, himself, was partly to blame for the accident—that was a lot harder than the run.

Maybe no one else would ever understand that.

He watched the darkened houses and the quiet sidewalks of the small town as the van passed by. He was thinking about Martin, how the guy knew basketball like the back of his hand; and the expression on his face when Jamie gave him the Dalhousie University team uniform. Man, what a feeling it'd be to wear a varsity basketball uniform.

Jay turned to his father. "Hey Dad, you ever hear of a basketball player called Spud Webb?"

Other books you'll enjoy in the Sports Stories series

Baseball

❏ *Baseball Crazy* by Martyn Godfrey #10
Rob Carter wins an all-expenses-paid chance to be bat boy at the Blue Jays spring training camp in Florida.

❏ *Slam Dunk* by Steven Barwin #23
The Raptors are going co-ed, but Mason and his friends aren't sure how they feel about it.

❏ *Shark Attack* by Judi Peers #25
The East City Sharks have a good chance of winning the county championship until their arch rivals get a tough new pitcher.

❏ *Hit and Run* by Dawn Hunter and Karen Hunter #35
Glen Thomson is a talented pitcher, but as his ego inflates, team morale plummets. Will he learn from being benched for losing his temper?

❏ *Power Hitter* by C. A. Forsyth #41
Connor's summer was looking like a write-off. That is, until he discovered his secret talent.

❏ *Out of Bounds* by Sylvia Gunnery # 70
When the Hirtle family's house burns down, Jay is forced to relocate and switch schools. He has a choice: sacrifice a year of basketball or play on the same team as his arch-rival Mike.

Basketball

❏ *Fast Break* by Michael Coldwell #8
Moving from Toronto to small-town Nova Scotia was rough, but when Jeff makes the school basketball team he thinks things are looking up.

❏ *Camp All-Star* by Michael Coldwell #12
In this insider's view of a basketball camp, Jeff Lang encounters some unexpected challenges.